THE SCOURGE OF BLACK ISLE
HIGHLAND HEALERS BOOK 3
Published by Keira Montclair
Copyright © 2021 by Keira Montclair

Printed in the USA.

Cover Design and Interior Format
© KILLION
THE
GROUP, INC.

THE SCOURGE OF BLACK ISLE

OF

HIGHLAND ⬩ HEALERS 3

KEIRA MONTCLAIR

CHAPTER ONE

Summer 1292, Black Isle in the Highlands of Scotland

GISELA MATHESON GASPED then pulled hard on the reins of her galloping steed as soon as she caught sight of a MacKinnie plaid in the distance. Her joy, so abundant on her ride with Padraig Grant, transformed to intense, immobilizing fear in the matter of a moment. She couldn't stop the fright that coursed through her, no matter how she tried to brush it off.

Heart-stopping fear was her normal response to the man known as the Scourge of Black Isle.

"What's wrong?" Padraig asked, pulling his black horse abreast of hers. His brown hair fell back over his shoulders, framing his handsome face, the concern in his gray eyes so evident that it squeezed her heart just a wee bit.

"Naught," she replied, turning away from him. "I thought I saw some riders ahead, and you know we cannot get caught. I'll race you back." She flicked the reins, and her horse jumped into action with a whinny of delight, turning around and heading back in the direction they'd just come. She'd have to try to outrun Padraig to keep the MacKinnie patrol from seeing them together.

Padraig's voice carried to her, asking her to stop, but her inclination to save her own skin overpowered her desire to wallow in the attention of her lover, spurring her faster.

"Gisela!" Padraig yelled, doing his best to stay abreast of her. "Slow down. Why so fast? What's wrong?"

She couldn't tell him exactly why she fled so swiftly. Curse it that the man knew her so well that he could detect her feelings from a furtive glance on horseback. True, she'd informed him that she was formally betrothed, an action her father had taken long before his death, and a state she detested. She hoped the problem with the curse, when Clan Matheson had lost half its members and its laird to a well poisoned by a jilted lover, had changed everything.

But she wasn't about to meet Donald MacKinnie in the middle of a forest to find out how he felt about their betrothal. She never wished to see him again. Ignoring Padraig's pleas to stop, she sent her mount flying across the glade, praying the thick, verdant leaves of the forest would hide her trail, cursing herself for the vibrant purple and green Matheson plaid she wore. She could hardly blend in with the dark green of the forest, and her white horse wouldn't help.

Hoping she'd escaped the brute, she slowed as they approached Eddirdale Castle, the home of Clan Matheson, and stopped her horse not far from the gates, doing her best to ease her rapid breathing. Her dear brother Marcas, his dark, brooding looks and tall posture familiar to everyone, was talking with Alvery, one of his guards, but stopped to stare at her, his head tipping in that way he had of quietly questioning her behavior.

"I saw something that frightened me," she attempted to explain. "'Tis all, Marcas, naught more. I'm fine. I did, however, run into Padraig on my way back."

"And what exactly frightened you, dear sister? Had you gone too far, ignoring my warnings?" He moved closer to help her dismount.

"It was some beast in the woods. You know I hate them," she said, lifting her chin in an attempt to show her brother she was calm and in control and to hide her wee lie. It wasn't a complete lie. Donald had become a beast over the last few moons. No one seemed to know why.

Her attempt failed. She could tell by the look in her brother's eyes as he dismissed Alvery to focus on her.

Curse it all. Her brother was far too insightful, and she had hoped to get away before his keen perception uncovered all in front of Padraig.

"You'll not fool me with your lie. What happened in truth?" Marcas cracked a slight smile as if to let her know he was on to her but wasn't angry about her attempt to slip him a tale.

Padraig came up behind her, dismounting but saying nothing, thankfully.

"As I said, I ran into Padraig on my way back,

and he saw I was upset, so he followed me." She spoke loudly enough for Padraig to hear her explanation, hinting for him to be quiet. She was spinning her story as she thought of it. She did not need Padraig revealing her tendency for creative storytelling.

"I tried to tell you to stop so I could see what had caused your flight, but you ignored me, Gisela. Why?" Padraig stared at her, awaiting an answer.

"I have my reasons, and I need not give them to either of you." She attempted a haughty departure, but the sound of horses' hooves stilled her.

Marcas drawled, "I'm guessing we're about to meet the beast who startled you."

Gisela spun around, and the blood drained from her face. Drat if it wasn't her betrothed, Donald MacKinnie, riding straight for them. His long, curly blond hair and blue eyes attracted many lasses, but he'd changed, and it was enough of an alteration in his personality for her to wish to end the betrothal, though she had yet to come up with a sound reason to declare herself free of him. She'd pushed her brothers to allow her to end it, especially after one of their servants, Thebe, had told them she'd seen him striking another lass, but they reminded her that betrothals were not ended on a whim.

Donald made a motion for his men to stop, then jumped down, coming to stand directly in front of her. Nodding at Marcas, he took two more steps toward her, his large frame towering over her, his ice-blue eyes boring into her.

She would not hide from him, nor would she allow him to think he intimidated her. Truth was, he *did* intimidate her, but she'd not show it.

As soon as he was close enough, he grabbed the underside of Gisela's arm, one of those painful, pinching holds he favored. What had transformed him into such a cruel ogre? He hadn't been that way until recently. How she hated this man.

His voice dripped venom. "What were you doing out with another man? Are you trying to cuckold me before we even say our vows?"

He let go of her arm and moved to Padraig, his hands firmly planted on his hips. Padraig was nearly as tall as the lout, but the Grant warrior looked more powerful, more muscular. Donald's frame had begun to carry a bit more fat than muscle. Padraig stood his ground.

"You're betrothed to this man?" Padraig glared at her quickly, but then blinked away his surprise. Marcas stepped closer, and she knew why. Her dearest brother was forever her protector. Padraig continued, blast it all. Could he not end his questions? "I'd heard mention of it, but I thought the betrothal had been called off. Is that not true, Gisela? Have you not canceled it, Marcas?"

At a loss for words, she looked from one man to the next, flustered by so much maleness in one small group. True, she wished out of the betrothal, but she hadn't discussed it formally with Donald, nor had her brother. There was a way to handle betrothals, and they'd failed miserably at it.

How she'd hoped ignoring it would cause it to go away. "Donald, I am not seeing this man. He is a cousin to my brother's new wife. It would please me if we could discuss our betrothal at a later time. Mayhap Marcas can arrange for a meeting with your sire."

Padraig took two steps back, and her belly clenched. He was as afraid of Donald as she was. Donald grabbed her arm again and yanked her up next to him, as if to declare her his property.

Property he could do with as he pleased. This would be her life as his wife.

She'd been wrong about Padraig. He had taken those steps back to clear the space so he could draw his sword.

"Take your hands from the lady. You're hurting her. I don't give a shite if she's your betrothed or not." The clench in his jaw told her he would not back down, no matter what Donald said.

Were Padraig's feelings for her so strong that he would be this protective?

Her youngest brother Shaw came out of nowhere to join them, probably drawn by the ring of the sword being unsheathed. He stood at their brother's side and said, "MacKinnie, take your hands from my sister."

Marcas, his eyes furious, declared, "Do as he says, or I'll let the Grant warrior do as he chooses."

"And we'll join him," Shaw added. "Every day you become more of a bastard. What the hell has happened to you?"

Donald smiled, releasing her arm slowly, but not before he leaned over and left a slimy kiss on her lips. "She's still mine, Matheson, and if you call off our marriage, you'll incite a clan war. I don't think you're in any position to fight, given all the men you lost to the curse."

"We heard a rumor that you are guilty of beating a woman. 'Tis true, MacKinnie?" Her brother Ethan was one to always tell the truth of a matter. He presently leaned over the curtain wall to pose his question, needing to yell it too loudly, to Donald. Gisela peered out of the corner of her eye to catch his response.

He only smiled. "I would never beat my betrothed, and you should know such a thing. Nor have I beaten any other woman. You insult my honor as a MacKinnie to ask such a thing. Where did you hear such lies?"

"'Twas merely a rumor. We'll not reveal the source, but Ethan has good reason to ask. We do not care to ever find our sister beaten." Marcas stood with his hands on his hips, his gaze not leaving Donald's. Gisela considered it a warning.

Would Donald feel the same?

"When she's my wife, you need not worry about her again. She'll belong to me, not you. And the number of guards you have left after the curse will not do anything to stop me taking her. Or do you and your minuscule group wish to challenge me now?" He leaned his head back and laughed. "As if you had any chance of besting me and my two friends."

"You'd be surprised, MacKinnie. Leave her be. We'll contact your sire and arrange a meeting to discuss the agreement later. Not here, not now, while we stand in front of our gates for all to hear. This is not the place to have a private negotiation, nor a battle." Marcas drew his own sword to back up his words.

Gisela looked at Donald, her belly flipping wildly at the thought of marriage to him. True, he was a handsome man, his blond hair golden in the sun, his blue eyes beautiful, but she hated everything else about him.

When he'd courted her, every word from his mouth had been sweet but empty, chosen blindly without thinking. He even told her he loved her blue eyes once.

Her eyes were green.

She guessed the man was so vain that he'd thought of his own eyes with that comment instead of hers.

And now his actions revealed his true nature. And it wasn't sweet. Perhaps that was why she now struggled to accept Padraig's flirting compliments.

"I'll have a word with my betrothed before I go. Alone. If you allow this, I'll accept that we'll make a final decision at Clan MacKinnie within a sennight." He crossed his arms, accentuating the muscles bulging in his upper arms. She caught him admiring himself, perhaps measuring his arms' circumference.

A vain man for certain.

When she heard the word "alone," she shot her brothers a look of fear, begging them not to agree. He'd likely cause a bruise, adding to the one she could already feel from his grip on her arm.

Marcas caught her look and said, "Not alone. I'll not let you close to her without protection.

I'll be near at hand. Over there near the curtain wall where no one else is."

Donald grumbled but reluctantly agreed with a nod. "You only, Chief." Marcas led them over, forcing Gisela in front of him so Donald couldn't reach her. She knew the way her brother's mind worked, and she was grateful for it.

Once they stood apart from the others, Donald jabbed his finger at her, almost poking her eye. "You will not embarrass me by consorting with other men."

Marcas slapped his hand down. "I'll control my sister's behavior. You control your own, or I'll send you off Matheson land. And if you don't leave fast enough, I'll put you on a spit and roast you. Seems you've put on enough lard to feed my entire clan."

"One more insult, and you'll feel the strength of my sword arm." Donald's voice rose to a bellow, his ire increasing the longer he remained on Matheson land. "As to your sister, I'll give you your wish and wait for you to come to MacKinnie land, but you will pay for insulting me and my clan." The fury in his eyes served as a promise to her. To think she'd thought him a fine catch in her younger years. Once they were betrothed, she'd learned what a mean bastard he was.

Several ago at a festival, she'd been guilty of flirting with him, drawn by his strength and good looks. He'd probably gone home and told his father he wished to claim her as his own. Her father, for some unknown reason, had agreed to it two years later. She'd thought Donald handsome and decent, so she hadn't argued, but she'd been young and foolish then. She hadn't known much about him, though his temperament had appeared to be mild back then.

Either she'd been wrong, or Donald had changed, and not for better.

Furious with all of them, Donald spun on his heel and stalked toward his horse. His two companions had never dismounted, and they rode off together.

She waited until he was far down the path and well out of earshot before she spoke. "Marcas, we have to end this betrothal. I completely forgot about it for a while, because of the sickness and losing so many people we loved. When I heard the rumor about his tendency to beat women, it all came back. I can't spend my life with such a man. I don't wish to feel his ire."

Marcas shook his head. "You should know better. The rumor came from someone who has a penchant for gossip, so we cannot take her word for it. Slapping a woman and beating her are two different things, though I'd not discuss it with him, but you know how Thebe exaggerates."

"I don't care to be slapped or beaten." She crossed her arms and glared at her brother.

"You are right and 'tis not worth discussing." Her brother held his hands up to her, knowing he shouldn't have mentioned the full details. "Aye, the betrothal was forgotten and delayed, but never officially canceled. I wish I understood why Papa arranged it. It's wrong, I see that now, and Papa would, too. But because we don't have proof of his cruelty, we'll have to find out the truth, something we can show his sire in order to cancel the betrothal. Chief MacKinnie won't believe his son hurts women without proof."

"You think Thebe lies?" Thebe was one of their trusted housemaids, but she was known for her wagging tongue. "Being a gossip does not mean 'tis a lie, but perhaps something she spreads without complete knowledge of it."

"I believe there is some truth to what she said, but we'll have to investigate the matter more thoroughly before we go to MacKinnie land. I would not subject you to such a callous, cruel husband. I'll find a way to put an end to this contract that will satisfy all involved parties. Until then, enjoy yourself."

He escorted her back to Shaw and Padraig.

She whispered, "Many thanks to you, Marcas. You know I adore you."

He rolled his eyes as he stepped away, but he stopped to glance over his shoulder. "Until we get this sorted, keep your lips away from my sister, Grant." Then he grinned. He led the group inside the gates to the courtyard.

Gisela breathed a sigh of relief once she was inside the safety of the castle wall. The gray stone rose fifteen feet high, multiple small, thatched huts nestled against the wall with work buildings surrounding the courtyard. She and Padraig led their horses toward the stable on the right while Shaw followed Marcas straight ahead into the keep proper, never minding the flock of fowl scattering before him.

Gisela wasn't surprised at all to find Thebe hurrying toward them from some hiding place near the gate.

"What happened?" the maidservant asked, all eager curiosity.

Thebe was known for not just her wagging tongue but for knowing everything that happened among the clans, so Gisela decided to keep quiet. "Naught important. Donald was being too rude, 'tis all it was."

Thebe scowled, glancing at Padraig then back to her, but Gisela didn't add anything more. She did not want speculation about her betrothal to spread all over the Isle.

Nonie came along as though she knew Thebe would be trying to pry information out of them. "Will you come inside, Gisela? I'm about to feed Tiernay and Kara, and they're asking for you."

More than glad to oblige the housekeeper, who helped care for her wee niece and nephew, she replied, "Of course. I'll be right in."

Kara and Tiernay were Marcas's bairns from his first wife, who had died from the curse, the result of her jilted lover poisoning their main well. The curse had taken half of their clan before Brigid and her cousins had discovered the source and put an end to their heaving sickness. Gisela had done all she could to help the wee ones adjust to their loss, but having Brigid Ramsay as their new stepmother had eased their pain very much.

Thebe bustled off either to find another source of gossip or to some task, and Nonie headed back into the keep, giving Gisela just enough time to

whisper to Padraig. "Now y⟨
must be careful."

Padraig smiled and said, " ⟨
challenge."

"Please don't challenge h⟨
see another morn."

"I didn't say this day. I'll ⟨
but I'll not allow him to g⟨⟩
you that way. 'Tis a promise." Then he winked.

She was doomed.

CHAPTER TWO

———◆———

PADRAIG GRANT, SON of Robbie and Caralyn Grant, glanced across the great hall from where he stood next to the hearth, the crowd trickling out after the evening meal and a few rounds of ale, only to catch Gisela's gaze upon him. The Matheson brothers and their guardsmen had stuffed themselves and imbibed enough to put half of them to sleep, but Padraig had not indulged as much as the others. The group began to break apart, the guards exiting the hall to leave the family to their nightly rituals before they found their own sleeping spots.

The bairns would be dressed in their bedclothes, while Marcas and Shaw shared tales of old battles from their sire's times or stories for the bairns to enjoy. His smile widened as his sweet lass sauntered across the hall toward him, swinging her hips just so, until his growing arousal underneath his plaid threatened to embarrass him.

He bent at the waist, sweeping his arm in front of him, and called out to her. "My lady, you are truly the loveliest of all." Indeed she was, her long brown hair falling in waves down her back unplaited, her green eyes sparkling with the same glee he'd seen on their ride through the forest until they'd been interrupted. She wore a dark green gown that accentuated her eyes and her generous curves in just the right places, but his favorite part was the freckles that danced across her nose and her high cheekbones, evidence of how much she enjoyed the outdoors.

He glanced to either side to be sure his female cousins, Brigid, Jennet, and Tara, were not close enough to overhear what he had to say to her, but they were not. He moved closer to her with a smile, clicking his boots against the stone floor as he waited for her approach. He wasn't far from the door and wondered if he could convince her to go for a stroll this eve, tipping his head as a hint to what he hoped she would do. Gisela came along beside him, then to his surprise passed him, giving him her best come-hither look over her shoulder. He followed, curious as to what *she* was about. She led him out the door and into the courtyard, the cool breeze pleasant after the stale air inside, still redolent with the aroma of roasted pig.

As he followed her into the night, his heart nearly sang out with delight at what he knew would come his way. An epiphany hit Padraig Grant right between the eyes. This beautiful, witty, clever woman strolling in front of him, her fabulous backside swinging provocatively, was going to change his life—forever. They passed the group of guardsmen, intoxicated enough to ignore the couple and focus on their discussion of a recent battle, something he appreciated. He had to admit he'd been surprised at how powerful his feelings of jealousy had been when confronted with Donald MacKinnie touching the lass in front of him.

He'd wished to pummel him until the man wouldn't have been able to mount his own horse, which was ridiculous because Padraig didn't often think of violence before considering other alternatives to handling situations. Whatever hold the lass had on him, it wasn't anything he'd lose easily.

He couldn't say how he knew. Only that he had a gut feeling about their relationship, and he knew anyone in Clan Grant would tell him to follow it.

"Padraig," she whispered over her shoulder without slowing her walk. "Your smile seems intended to entice, I think. Give you that look to every lass you meet?" Gisela asked, her long brown waves falling down her back, her green eyes dancing with promise in the light of the courtyard torches.

"Nay, never." He held his hand over his heart and feigned a fall to the ground, her laughter music to his ears. He bolted back upright, his pouting expression demonstrating how her question wounded him. "How could you think it were so? You are truly the most beautiful woman I've ever seen."

Her gaze narrowed at him as she stopped to wait for him. "Is that all you see in me, you daft, sweet-talking man?"

"Nay," he said softly, getting serious for a moment. He tugged her with him into a secluded area at the edge of the courtyard. He leaned in close, kissing her lips lightly, just to see if she would reject him.

She did not.

He whispered, "I see a bright, loyal woman who is compassionate and loving to her clan. Your dedication to setting your clan to rights after the dreaded curse is most admirable. But even the most hard-working woman must have some fun."

He leaned down and took her lips with his again. She parted her lips quickly, letting him inside, giving him a taste of her sweet mouth that he'd not soon forget. Her response delighted and surprised him. Their tongues mated, and he couldn't stop the growl coming from deep in his chest as he wrapped his arms around her, tugging her close enough that their bodies melded. He didn't even care if she felt his blatant hardness through their clothing.

He wanted Gisela Matheson more than anyone else he'd ever met. Powerless against her honeyed lips, he angled his mouth to delve deeper, but she ended the kiss too quickly.

She tipped her head back to look up at him. "Much as I enjoy your attentions, my lord, I should not carry on so. There are some people, as you know, who I don't wish to be a witness to my actions. I fear there may be gossipmongers about watching our every move."

He knew exactly who and what she meant. She was afraid Thebe's tale-telling would reach

Donald MacKinnie, rousing his ire again.

"Why do you think Thebe would betray you? She seems to be your friend," he stated as he escorted her out around the back part of the wall and into the village, hoping to put an end to her worries. Away from the light of the castle torches, there was less chance they'd be seen. "Has she no loyalty to your clan?"

Gisela sighed and flipped some stray hairs back over her shoulder. "Thebe used to be a member of Clan Milton. At the time, she claimed to love Donald, but then once the curse was resolved, she asked to join Clan Matheson, claiming a need to get far away from the man. She told Nonie that Donald was the only one for her, but he had no interest in her, so she wished to move as far away from him as possible. Nonie told me because she knew we were betrothed, though I'd tried to forget it. Regardless of that, she hasn't been here long enough to have loyalty to our clan."

"Has he ever courted you, or is the betrothal in name only?"

She took Padraig's hand and tugged him over to a tree. "Aye, a year or more ago, I did like Donald. He seemed a sweet man. Obviously, he's good-looking…"

"Hush now," Padraig said, his eyes widening. "Tell me you do not think him more handsome than the man standing in front of you." Padraig dropped her hand and stepped away from her, striking several different poses to show how strong and handsome he was. "I'm sure I must be much better-looking. Stronger. Nicer lips to kiss." He winked at her, and she answered with a giggle.

"Of course you are far more handsome. But I did see a possibility with him at first. After the curse was broken, he came by to visit, make sure I had survived, but he'd changed. He was mean to me, and I didn't like it." She looked into the distance, as if remembering the visit. "He seemed angry, he disparaged our clan over the curse when it was clearly not our fault, struck his horse with some object he held in his hand that I that I couldn't help but react to, my voice nearly a scream. But the worst was that I feared he was about to strike me. He stopped when he realized my brothers surrounded me." She stared at the ground for a moment before lifting her head to explain her thoughts. "He never mentioned the betrothal, which was odd. And the way he looked at me gave me shivers. "I don't understand it. At first it troubled me, but now I'm frightened of what he might do. He's not a man to be taken lightly."

"He'll do nothing to harm you as long as I'm near. Stop thinking about him. Accept it as making way for the man meant for you. Put an end to your worries. I'm from Clan Grant, born and raised to be a Grant warrior, and I'd be more than happy to challenge that bastard you're so worried about." Padraig didn't mention that he wasn't the strongest of the Grant warriors, though he was indeed a better swordsman than many. But among the warriors of the Grant family, he did not stand out, no matter how many hours he trained.

"I'll force him from my mind for you, Padraig." She pushed against his chest and said, "You'll not fight my battles for me. Do not forget that I am mistress of the clan, so I must be strong and virtuous." They continued their stroll around the outside of the village located behind the castle wall. The castle had been built so closely to the coastline of Beauly Firth that there wasn't much room for the number of huts they'd needed before the curse had taken half their clan.

"I thought Brigid was mistress of the clan." Brigid had married Marcas just that spring, and since Marcas was laird, that made her mistress according to the clan practices he knew.

Gisela flashed a quick look of guilt, but she recovered quickly. "Of course she is. But I wish to assist her in her new role. She asked for my help, and I'm helping Marcas's bairns get to know her as well. Though Tiernay and Kara seem to be quite happy."

They made their way back to the courtyard, sneaking in the back entrance to avoid the group of guards who'd turned quite raucous and could be heard over the curtain wall. Padraig leaned forward and kissed her cheek. "I'll accept that you must behave well in public, but lass, I want more of you. More conversation, more laughter, more kisses. Shall I fall to my knees and beg you?"

Her laughter echoed across the courtyard. "Nay, do not make a scene, Padraig Grant."

"All right. I'll escort you inside, mistress."

Padraig held the door open for her, and she

made her way inside the great hall, where the remaining members of the household were a bit quieter than the group in the courtyard.

They moved over to the hearth, where those who remained gathered in quiet conversation, and Padraig had to force himself to drop his hand, which he held protectively against the arch of Gisela's back.

The group made a pretty picture. Brigid, Jennet, and Tara together, the men around them. Ethan sat behind Jennet, Marcas stood leaning against the mantle, and Shaw at the end by Tara.

The conversation stopped dead as soon as they entered. Gisela looked around the hall, empty except for the group by the hearth. "I see you were talking about me."

Padraig took in the serious looks on Marcas's and Shaw's faces and figured she was right. Ethan's countenance rarely changed, so it was hard to get any inkling from him.

This was a Matheson family discussion, so he held his tongue. Better to hear the brothers out before he spoke.

Marcas held his hand out toward the one remaining seat closest to the hearth. "Have a seat, Gisela. We'd be glad to discuss this with you."

Padraig followed her over to the chair and couldn't stop himself from standing behind her in a show of support. He had no idea how their family discussions usually went.

"We've come to a decision and plan to act on it this week. A decision you need to be aware of, sister, since it concerns you."

Gisela nearly came out of her chair, but Padraig settled his hands on her shoulders, encouraging her to listen. "You've not heard them yet, have you, lass?"

She glanced back over her shoulder at him, her face full of both fury and fear, if that were possible. "Go ahead, Marcas."

Marcas waggled his brow at Padraig. "He's a wise man. My thanks for listening to him."

She cleared her throat but said nothing, so Padraig took a step back.

"After careful consideration, Ethan, Shaw, and I have decided to visit Clan MacKinnie on the morrow with the intention of ending your betrothal."

Gisela relaxed, letting out an audible breath, and gave her brother a small smile. "My thanks. I'll be pleased to go along and see Donald's reaction."

Shaw barked, "Och, you are no' going, lass."

This time, Padraig let her go when she bolted out of her chair. "'Tis my life you are speaking of. If you decide to make some bargain, I'll be there."

Marcas held his hand up to her. "We'll strike no bargain that will have Donald marrying you. Much has changed in the years since Papa agreed to this betrothal, and Donald is no suitable man for you or any woman now. While I'll try not to mention the rumors we've heard about Donald's cruelty to women, I will if I must. But let me ask you this, dear sister. You seem to have a penchant for the man behind you, but I don't think you are of a mind to become betrothed to him yet, are you?"

She turned around to stare at Padraig and shook her head, her eyes wide. "Nay, we just met, Marcas. Please don't put that pressure on him. 'Tis most unfair."

"Agreed. My apologies, Grant, for putting you on the spot. Should you change your mind, 'twould be most expedient if you let me know as soon as your feelings are certain."

Tara said, "Padraig will make you a fine husband."

Padraig wished Tara wouldn't speak as if the marriage were already arranged, but he kept his mouth closed. With all the brothers present, he wished neither to deny her words nor discuss at all what kind of husband he might make. He was not yet ready for marriage, though if he were, he would choose Gisela and no other.

"If you are not willing to announce a betrothal to Padraig, Gisela, then my advice is to stay away from him for a while," Marcas said. He looked to Padraig again. "In fact, while we've appreciated your assistance, mayhap 'tis time for you to take your leave, Grant."

"Not yet," Shaw said. "Not until we find out if the MacKinnies plan a direct attack."

Brigid's shock showed on her face. "Would they do such a thing?"

Marcas stepped close to her and placed a hand on her back as if to soothe her. "They could, but I think they won't. Attacking a clan after what we've been through would be dishonorable, but some were prepared to do it before. They considered our lands ripe for takeover with so many sick or dead. 'Twas only fear of the curse that kept them at bay long enough for us to rebuild, and the help of Logan Ramsay and his band of archers. We cannot forget how the other clans viewed us before Clan Ramsay came to our assistance. The MacKinnies could have been one of the clans willing to attack with the Miltons."

Ethan added, "MacKinnie will not attack unless they truly wish to take over our clan. They'll not do it yet. Donald won't take the broken betrothal well, but I expect he'll retaliate in a different way."

Marcas nodded. "I think you're right, Ethan. Gisela, you shouldn't step outside the curtain wall until Donald has accepted this. Another reason why you'll not be going with us. We won't give him the opportunity to try to steal you away. He is not beneath such underhanded behavior. We'll be doing things differently for a while."

"Differently?" Gisela asked.

"Carefully," Shaw said.

"And if we must, Brigid will send a message to her sire to bring a force of Ramsays to help protect the castle," Jennet said.

"Would he do that?" Gisela asked, looking to Brigid. "He just left after the near tragedy with Jennet, after all."

Brigid actually snorted as she looked at Jennet, who laughed.

"My father loves to battle," her sister-in-law said. "He doesn't even need an invitation."

"I'll agree with that," Padraig said. "I can bring Grant warriors if you wish, but Uncle Logan can be here much faster than the Grant warriors."

Ethan said, "Logan is your uncle, Padraig? How?" The other man looked as if he were counting the family relations in his head.

The four cousins all broke into laughter at the same time. Jennet leaned over and kissed his cheek. "You are correct, love of mine, that they're not blood relatives, but rules don't apply here. All the Grants call him uncle. We are all so close, and have been for years, that it has always been that way."

Shaw looked at the group of cousins, scratching his jaw. "Why can your father get here faster, Brigid? Grant land is closer."

Padraig chuckled. "Because Logan Ramsay makes Kyle Maule train Ramsay men to run, too. They are specially trained to move fast, and the archers are the fastest, most efficient force you'll ever see. There are far *more* Grant warriors, over a thousand, but we train for strength, with the aim to be powerful swordsmen. Our horses are warhorses, specially bred and trained for battle. Neither our horses nor men can move as fast as the Ramsay archers. And they move very fast indeed, making up for the difference in distance."

"'Tis quite a brilliant strategy." Ethan crossed his arms and tapped his foot as he thought. They all turned to look at him, knowing he had more to say. "You are close allies. Together, you are the most powerful force in all of England and the land of the Scots, I would guess."

Jennet looked at Brigid, then Tara, and finally Padraig before announcing, "You are exactly correct, Ethan."

Marcas said, "But we'll not relax over this. After we leave MacKinnie land, we'll need to be extra careful."

"But why?" Gisela asked. "We'll have help if we want it." Her arm swept toward the group.

"I'll tell you why," Shaw said. "Because Grants might be stronger and Ramsays faster, but Donald is sneakier."

Padraig couldn't argue that point. And neither did anyone else.

CHAPTER THREE

GISELA SAT IN the great hall near the hearth, helping three-year-old Kara dress while Brigid fed Tiernay, who at just over a year, couldn't quite handle his own spoon in the porridge yet. The hall proved to be the warmest place to dress the young ones, something Gisela had started during the curse, and Brigid hadn't changed the habit.

The truth was Brigid had done nearly everything with the bairns the same way Gisela had. Perhaps it was part of the reason she was so fond of Marcas's new wife.

The guards had eaten and left, leaving the hall nearly empty. Her mind was on the events of the day before, an image of Donald's finger in her face particularly persistent.

"Are you anxious about what will happen this day?" Brigid asked.

"Aye." Gisela fussed with Kara's long brown hair, separating it into strands to plait. The men had already left for MacKinnie land, and they wouldn't return for at least two hours, something that would test her patience more than anything.

"I would have liked to go, but I think Marcas is correct. Donald is a sneaky man. I'm glad he left some guards here."

"Ethan will protect us. I am not worried," Jennet added, coming down the staircase. "Gisela, would you like me to take Kara so you can relax? You will surely be anxious until they return."

Not dress Kara? "Nay, I am happy to finish with my sweet niece," she said, giving Kara a kiss on the top of her head. "You love Auntie Gisela, do you not, sweeting?"

"Aye, Auntie 'Ela, but you pulling my hair too tight. Ow." Her hand went up to protect her head.

Gisela eased up on the weaving of Kara's hair. "Sorry, sweetie. I'll fix it."

"Nay, Bwigid do it, pweez."

Gisela dropped her hands from Kara as if the wee lassie had slapped them and stared at Brigid, aghast. She'd hurt her dear niece.

Tara took over feeding Tiernay while Brigid moved to Kara, who promptly announced, "My new mama doesn't pull my hair. I wuv Mama Bwigid like you, Auntie 'Ela."

The loss of Freda, Marcas's first wife, to the curse had been a blow to the whole household. And then the man who'd poisoned the well had taken Kara right out of Gisela's arms while they'd slept through their own fevers. He'd thought to keep something of Freda, his former lover, for himself, since he couldn't have the woman he'd loved past madness. But the worst part was the bastard had snuck into the keep in the middle of the curse when they'd all been so sickly. He'd stolen her away from Gisela's own arms where they'd slept on a pallet near the hearth, both sick with fevers.

Gisela had never forgiven herself for that, even though she knew the bastard was entirely at fault. Kara had been in her care when she'd been stolen away, and she'd never awakened because of her own sickness. How could that be?

She and her brothers had lost both parents to the curse also, and Gisela had vowed to take over for her mother, be the mistress of the clan and help Marcas rebuild as laird. Then Brigid had come along. They'd fallen in love and married quickly.

She knew it was the best for the clan. They needed a strong leader and a new mistress. Brigid was a healer and had known little about running the keep, so Gisela had taught her what she needed to know.

But now, with Brigid established, their gifted cook Jinny in the kitchen, and Nonie at the ready, Gisela hadn't found much to do. She'd been little more than a girl before the curse. No longer. It was past time to find her role as a woman.

So Gisela had adjusted by focusing on her niece and nephew. She had much to make up for to wee Kara, who'd been tied to a tree until her tender skin had torn and bled, so she spent much of her time catering to her needs.

Of course, Brigid was great at being a mother, too. Nay. She needed to rephrase that. Brigid was a wonderful mother to both children. Wee Tiernay would never remember his real mother, and Kara would lose much of her memory of Freda. They were both quickly coming to accept and love Brigid.

As it should be. Dismissed from service with Kara, Gisela slumped into a chair by the hearth and stared into the flames.

Tara came and sat next to her. "It's good you'll not be marrying Donald. Though she might fuss when you plait her hair, Kara loves and relies on you. And Tiernay, too, the way wee bairns do."

"Aye, I know they do. And I'll never leave them as long as they need me." Her eyes misted with tears at the memory of all they'd been through. She'd often worried if the wee lass especially would be marred for life, but she'd proved to be more resilient than Gisela would have guessed. Kara was as sweet and happy as could be.

"What about Padraig? Where does he fit in?"

She whipped her head up to look at Tara. Such a bold question. "I'm not sure. He's fun to be with. He takes my mind off Donald." She twirled a strand of her long hair around her finger, winding and winding away, intentionally containing her other thoughts. He was a masterful kisser, always considerate and sweet, someone she knew she could depend on. "His personality is wonderful simply because he can always make me laugh, especially when I need it most."

"What if Padraig wants more?"

She scrunched her face up, still winding her hair, perhaps even a little faster. "Padraig won't be interested in me that way. It could never be."

Tara arched a brow at her in question.

"Padraig would never stay here, and I can never leave my nie— I mean, my brothers. We need to be together. Padraig is a wanderer, so he tells me. He says he'll never settle down in one place."

"But Shaw told me you'd like to travel."

She let her hair go, dropped her hands into her lap, and stared into the flames. "Before the curse changed everything, aye. I wanted to travel to Edinburgh. To see more of the land."

"But that's changed?"

"Aye, we must stand together now. Rebuild our clan. Make Mama and Papa proud." Her gaze traveled back to Kara. "Too much has happened too fast, if you wish the truth. I don't know what will happen one day to the next."

"None of us do, but you have had an enormous amount of change in your life. Why don't you just focus on the moment? Fretting about the future will do you no good. First see what your brothers report about their meeting with Donald. I'm sure they'll return with good news, and you'll be able to go on with your life, no worries at all."

"I hope you are correct, Tara. My thanks for the advice."

She stared into the flames again after Tara left. It didn't feel at all like good news would be coming.

It felt more like her world as she knew it was about to come to an end.

———— ◆ ————

Padraig held his horse back, staying behind the Matheson brothers as they neared MacKinnie Castle. From the outside, it didn't look like much, not nearly as large as most clan castles, and it didn't have the carvings in the parapets similar to Grant Castle's. Close in size to the castle his brother Roddy lived in with his wife Rose, it didn't look well maintained nor did it have any of the landscaping or beautiful floral displays of most others, thus missing a bright air of welcome.

The ride over had given him plenty of time to think, since the brothers chatted between themselves and the guards were mostly quiet.

He missed his brother. Perhaps when he moved on from here, he'd visit Roddy in the western Highlands. He'd been here for a long while and had to admit he'd enjoyed his time, but mostly because he'd enjoyed being with Gisela. Was that all about to change?

His next stop, when he thought about leaving a place, was never home, but always someplace a little farther on, a little different. He didn't admit to many that the reason he didn't live on Grant land was because he didn't belong. He wasn't the overpowering warrior the Grant men were supposed to be, and he'd honestly tired of working in the lists teaching men and lads the Grant method of fighting. The hours of drilling thrusts and blocks until his arms ached, then testing the guards to see who had the mettle and strength to hold up in battle had worn him down.

It just wasn't for him. Rather than reject his sire to his face, he wandered, wishing he could be someone like Logan Ramsay, who traveled as a spy. Always on the move. He loved seeing new people, new faces.

His other alternative? He supposed he could live with Roddy and his wife Rose, who'd taken in a whole pack of orphans and made their life in her family's castle on a beautiful sea loch, along with Roddy's best friend and right-hand man Daniel with his wife, Constance. Who knew who else they'd taken in along the way?

The idea had its advantages—lots of bairns, the stability of a lovely castle with some Grant guards for protection. But probably no lasses to hold his interest. Of course, he hadn't been especially interested in any lass in particular until Gisela. Going to visit his brother could be the best thing for him. With a little distance, he could learn his true feelings for Gisela. Was their relationship a passing fancy or something meant to be?

Unfortunately, Padraig liked lasses. Tall, short, round, giggly, quiet, he didn't care. They fascinated him. He enjoyed talking to them as much as he did making love to them. But other lasses never interested him the same way Gisela did. No other could hold his attention, draw his gaze, or warm his insides like Gisela.

Padraig had been known as quite a flirt with the lasses over the past couple of years, but he'd changed.

He curtailed the snort that begged to be let loose. He couldn't even fool himself into believing that bit of hogwash. True, if Gisela was interested in him, he could let go of any others because they truly held no deeper interest for him, but he did enjoy lasses, and the prospect of living in a castle with none was not the least bit appealing.

No matter his path, Gisela was about to get her freedom, and he wasn't ready for marriage any more than she seemed to be. Perhaps some time away would be best for both of them.

When he shook himself free of his thoughts, he realized they were nearly upon the MacKinnie castle's locked gates, the fortress even more dismal up front than he'd first thought. Taking a quick count of the number of guards visible, he was no longer worried they'd be attacked. They just didn't have the number available and ready to take on the Matheson group. A guard yelled out to them as they approached the castle. "State your business!"

"We're Marcas and Shaw Matheson, here to meet with your chief and with his son Donald," Marcas called back.

The guard disappeared to check with his chieftain. Marcas turned around and looked at Padraig. "Do you wish to attend the meeting with Shaw and me, or would you rather stay out here with the guards?"

"I'll go with you. Three swords are better than two."

Marcas's lips quirked in a barely contained smile, but Shaw's didn't, instead whispering, "Surely are."

The guard returned and said, "We'll open the gates to no more than three. Your guards stay out."

"Agreed," Marcas replied, dismounting. He gave Padraig a small nod to say he was welcome to join them.

He followed the two brothers inside the

courtyard. All became quiet as they strode past the villagers, who'd stopped what they were doing to stare at the intruders, the weaver giving them a hard look unlike the others. What had he heard? The short walk gave him a quick view of Clan MacKinnie's wealth. The castle was about equal to the Matheson's, but the roof of the buttery needed rethatching, and he caught a rat scurrying out of the grain storage, running toward the base of the keep, making him put his hand on the hilt of his sword.

The rat needed to stay the hell away from him, he thought as he wiggled his toes in his boots to be certain they were still protecting his feet.

They passed two men at the smithy's workshop, a guard testing a new sword with the swing of the weapon to test the feel and the weight while the smithy observed the practice. Padraig had to control the urge to chuckle at the small size of the sword and the difficulty the warrior appeared to have moving it.

It was a scene he'd never see on Grant land.

They stepped through the castle's door and were escorted up the staircase and into the chieftain's solar.

The chieftain, Fearchar MacKinnie, was an old man, his sons born late in life. As far as Padraig knew, he'd always been called simply MacKinnie, even before he'd taken over clan leadership from his sire. He sat at the end of a table, and Donald stood at his left side while another man stood behind them. The guards at the door remained outside, closing the door behind Padraig.

"Matheson, my sympathy for the loss of your parents and your wife. I received word of your recent marriage. A Ramsay lass speaks of great fortune for your clan. And if she is as good a healer as I've heard, you are indeed a lucky man."

"Aye, I married Logan Ramsay's youngest daughter, Brigid." Marcas stood with his shoulders squared. Tall and broad, he gave the impression of a chieftain who would not yield to anyone or anything. Padraig couldn't help but admire the man for stepping into his sire's shoes so young. Losing both parents and his wife had to have been devastating. Padraig couldn't blame Brigid for her attraction to the dark and powerful man. He knew in that moment that the chief of MacKinnie would not deter Marcas from his purpose.

MacKinnie narrowed his gaze at Marcas, judgment in his keen look. The man had gray hair and a long gray beard, and eyes that missed nothing. "You did not wait long to remarry. You don't believe in honoring the memory of the mother of your bairns?"

Marcas's tension radiated from his shoulders, but his voice remained steady. "You knew ours was not a love match. And my marital state is no concern of yours. We are here on other business, as I'm sure you're aware."

If the old man thought he could shake Marcas's confidence by embarrassing him or attempting to throw an accusation of guilt upon the young chieftain, he was wrong.

Donald grunted. Perhaps he'd hoped to

see Marcas yield to his father in this opening gambit, making it more likely he'd yield in their conversation about the betrothal as well. Padraig laughed to himself. The Mathesons would not change their minds, no matter what the MacKinnies said.

The chieftain pointed to chairs around the table. "Please sit. I'll have Dougal get you some refreshment."

"No need. We'll be quick with our business. You know my brother Shaw, and this"—he pointed to Padraig—"is my wife's cousin Padraig Grant." Marcas sat down opposite MacKinnie and gestured for the other two to join him, one on either side. That left Donald the only one standing.

Again, Padraig was impressed. He recognized the tactic from watching his uncle Alex—make your point but act as if it is unimportant, then allow your true meaning to sit with your opposite, giving them time to consider the most critical words. Or in this case, word—*Grant*.

Marcas had let MacKinnie know that besides the Ramsays, he had another powerful ally, Clan Grant.

"So you've gained two formidable allies with this marriage, both clans with numbers far exceeding ours."

"'Tis true that I consider them both allies."

"So why are you here?" Padraig guessed him to be a keen strategizer, judging by how quickly he picked up the consequences of Marcas's marriage to Brigid.

"As you know, our sister Gisela was betrothed by our father to your son Donald four or five years ago, I believe. Is that correct, Chief?"

"Aye, you are correct. 'Tis time for the betrothal to end and for the marriage to take place. Name your date."

Marcas's gaze never strayed to Donald but stayed on the chieftain. "As chieftain of Clan Matheson, I am breaking the betrothal. After the turmoil of the last few months, the match no longer suits my sister. Events such as we've lived through change a woman. And as for your son, he's a brute, and I won't allow him to come near my sister again, let alone marry her. I'm sure you've heard rumors about how your son treats women. I won't allow that kind of treatment of my sister."

Then he looked at Donald. "My apologies for this inconvenience, but I'm sure you'll easily find another, Donald. You've probably had numerous offers from other chieftains."

Donald's face turned so dark red that Padraig thought he would have a spell in front of them, but he managed to speak through gritted teeth. "I want Gisela. She's mine."

"Nay, she's not. She will not marry you, especially after I have seen the bruises you have caused. I have spoken." Marcas stood, ready to leave, but the chieftain stopped him.

"What is this truly about, Marcas? Every woman needs a bit of slapping to get them to mind your wishes, especially strong-minded ones. 'Tis not a reason to end a betrothal. Your sire is raging from his grave to have you defy his order."

Marcas shook his head. "Nay, he's not. I know my sire has seen how poorly they match now. He has been able to watch from Heaven every time they clash, and he has seen the bruising results of those exchanges. I've seen it myself, and I must protect my sister from a life she no longer wants. The decision stands."

"This is war," Donald declared. "And 'tis his fault." His finger came up abruptly, aimed directly at Padraig. "He's the one consorting with Gisela, telling her lies." Spittle flew from his angry lips as he spoke, on the verge of losing control.

Marcas shook his head. "This has nothing to do with Grant. She cannot live the type of life you offer her, and that is the only reason for my decision."

"She belongs to me. I'll do what I wish with her." His fist thumped his chest, but his other hand went to the side of his head, rubbing his knuckles across the surface.

"The hell you will," Shaw said, standing and leaning toward Donald. Padraig stood as well, emphasizing their unified front.

"Enough!" the MacKinnie chieftain yelled. "Sit, please. Let's discuss this with reason." The group calmed and took their seats again. "Now, Marcas, every lass needs to be put in her place. He's not the first to raise his hand to his betrothed or his wife. If she needs it, she'll get disciplined. Bruising will heal. And as for the rumors, they're just that. I'm sure Donald didn't hurt anyone else."

Marcas stood up again, set his hands on the table, and leaned forward, his voice dropping to a low, menacing tone. "Nay. Blows and bruises are no way to win a lass's respect. My sister will not be mistreated. The betrothal is over." Then he turned to leave, Shaw and Padraig following.

The three had nearly reached the door when Donald came barreling toward Padraig. He grabbed for him with one meaty paw, but Padraig was quicker, dodging and landing a solid punch to the side of his jaw, making an audible crack.

Donald roared, but his sire roared louder. "Donald! You'll stop now, or I'll take the whip to you myself."

Padraig stood loose and watchful, ready to throw a second punch, but he didn't need to. Apparently, his father would make good on his threats, because Donald stopped instantly, even taking a step backward. But anger still blazed in his expression.

"Matheson," the chief called after them. "We'll give you a few days to reconsider your decision. I understand the curse left you with many raw wounds. Follow that with the foolish witchery trial your brother was involved in, and I see you are ready for some calm and reason in your life. That much I'll give you. A sennight. You'll accept Donald within the sennight."

Donald stared at Padraig, pointed at him, and said, "You'll pay, Grant. You'll see."

Padraig just nodded. "Come for me whenever you like. We'll see who the stronger swordsman is."

"No swords. I'll taunt you first, then kill you with my bare hands." The bastard tipped his head back and grinned.

What the hell did that mean?

CHAPTER FOUR

———◆———

GISELA WAITED IN the great hall, seated in her favorite chair near the hearth. She held mending on her lap, but her hands were still. She was too distracted to make a single stitch. Brigid was cutting bandages for their healing chamber while Tara and Jennet worked at a table concocting some healing ointment.

Thebe came running into the room, nearly tripping when she stepped across the threshold. "They're back, and they don't look pleased."

Nonie barked, "Thebe, you'll not give your opinion on something you know naught about. This is none of your concern. Come with me to the kitchens." The housekeeper spun on her heel and went out the back door. Thebe cursed under her breath, but she followed.

Brigid said, "Pay her no mind. She's a gossip, plain and simple. The more she can rile people up, the happier she is. I have faith in your brothers."

"Thank goodness for Nonie. She is the best housekeeper ever," Tara said.

Gisela smiled, remembering how sweet the woman had been to her when she was just a wee lassie. "She is, and she's been here forever."

No more than a minute passed before the door opened, Shaw and Padraig entering with Marcas behind them. Marcas headed straight for Brigid, wrapped his arms around her and leaned into her, sighing deeply.

"Not a pleasant trip, husband?" she asked, letting him have his fill of whatever it was he needed from her touch.

"Nay, I've had better." He leaned back, then kissed her quickly. "I'm still adjusting to being chieftain. I'd have liked to strike one particular person dead on the spot, but I had to control myself, now that I speak for our clan."

"Who?" Gisela asked, her hand going to her throat. She prayed Padraig had not been the troublemaker.

"Donald, of course." He turned around, but kept a firm hold on Brigid's hand.

Jinny, the head cook, stuck her head in the door, and Brigid said, "Some refreshment for the men, please, Jinny." She nodded and disappeared.

"Tell me, please. What happened?" Gisela gripped the arms of her chair.

"I informed them that your betrothal is called off," Marcas said. "It should be in your past, and you need not worry about a wedding you don't wish for. They have not completely accepted it, Gisela, but after meeting with them and seeing evidence of Donald's temper, I'm more convinced than ever that you will not marry that man. He's changed. I've not seen him so belligerent in the past, and I'm glad we've seen his true character now instead of after the wedding."

"There must be more, Marcas. Telling him you were calling off the betrothal would not have shaken you so. Please tell me everything that happened and leave nothing out." She folded her hands in her lap, vowing not to rip every ribbon out of her gown while she waited for the full explanation.

"The chief gave us a sennight to change our minds," Marcas said. "He did not accept Donald's brutality as a reason to cancel a betrothal, but I insisted it was over."

Shaw and Marcas both glanced at Padraig, then Shaw explained, "Donald said you were his, and he promised vengeance against Padraig for stealing your affections."

Gisela felt the blood drain from her cheeks, and her finger went to her hair, finding a tendril to twirl. "And what if we don't change our minds? What kind of revenge is Donald planning?"

Twirl and twirl. That ultimatum could mean anything. A clan war. A bride-stealing. Stealing horses or cows or sheep or...

"He did not say, but Donald believes Padraig to be the cause of the issue." Shaw moved over to the hearth and leaned one hand against it, staring into the flames. "I'm not sure what to make of the whole thing. Marcas, I wish Da were here."

Padraig shrugged. "I'm not worried, Gisela. I'll fight him anytime. He's no bigger than I am, and he's flabby in spots. I doubt his sword skills are verra strong."

"I'd be wary," Shaw said, now pacing in front

of the fire.

"Why?" Padraig jerked his head around to face Gisela's brother. "He likes to talk about fighting, but not likely to act on his words, is he? He doesn't strike me as a skilled swordsman. He doesn't have the muscles in his body or the power in his arms."

"No," Marcas said. "Donald is not all talk. He may not have the sword skills of a Grant, but there are other ways to kill someone. If we don't agree to the wedding in a sennight, he'll retaliate in some way, no matter what his sire intends. He's gone strange in the head. Did you see how he rubbed his temple?" He looked from Shaw to Gisela, then back to Padraig. "He's not the same man he was a year ago. And they've had no curse thrust upon them. The question is what's caused the change?"

"You're imagining something that's not there. He's busy trying to think up some evil way to torture us," Shaw said. "Or you, Padraig. Do not dismiss his threat. While I don't think he'd move against our sister, he won't hesitate to target you. Consider him to be crafty. He won't come at you directly with a sword. Whatever he does will be sly and devious."

Gisela gasped, staring at Padraig, who seemed completely at ease, as if no threat hung over his head. "Oh, my Lord in Heaven." She stood up and rushed over to him. "You have to leave."

Shaw held his hand up to his sister. "Donald's sire and brother will keep him in line. Dougal is in line for the lairdship, not Donald. He'll not jeopardize his inheritance by letting Donald do something foolish."

Padraig's hands settled on her shoulders, and he met her gaze. "I'm not going to run away from him. It would hardly be an honorable answer to his challenge. I'll stay and meet him when he's ready. The man's no serious threat as a swordsman. I saw today that he's slow and unsteady on his feet. Please don't worry about me. The important thing is Marcas ended your betrothal. No matter the comment about changing your minds in a sennight, I don't think they'll take any action when you don't agree to the marriage. He'll forget you in time, though God knows I pity the next lass he sets his sights on. He's not easily distracted from his purpose."

Gisela couldn't stop the trembling in her hands. "You don't know Donald. He will do as he says."

Marcas cast a resigned glance Padraig's way. "She's right. Don't underestimate Donald MacKinnie. You must be aware at all times, Grant. I'll say again that you should consider leaving us for a time. Return when this is resolved."

"Please, Padraig? Go before he kills you. I promise to stay on Matheson land and not wander."

Padraig gave her a fierce look. "Grant men don't run, and we don't back down."

———— ♦ ————

Later that night, Padraig sat on the pallet in the small hut that he slept in just inside the curtain wall. He'd lived inside the castle for a while, but being that close to Gisela was too tempting, so he'd moved into one of the huts left empty by the curse. He thought about his clan and the warriors of his family—sire, uncles, brother, cousins. What would any of them do if a man like Donald threatened them?

They'd stand strong and wait for the attack, Grant warriors at their backs. If he'd left home under different circumstances, he'd send a message asking for a few of his clanmates to come and lend their swords to guarding against Donald's threat not only to him but Gisela. Whatever it took to repel Donald, however he chose to attack, and keep Gisela safe.

His sire would send them in a minute if he knew what he was up against, but because he'd left on a bad note, he didn't feel comfortable asking for help.

His father had wanted him to lead in the lists. Once Roddy and Braden had left, they'd needed someone strong to run the training of the youngest warriors. "I'm getting too old, Padraig. Your clan needs you." There were plenty of men to train, so they needed more than one or two seasoned warriors capable of instructing men and preparing them for battle. Grant boys and men were trained and ranked by their ability. Some were trained as guards for the noble family, some to protect the castle. Others were trained to be first on the battlefield. Padraig had trained the youngest in the lists, testing their abilities, bringing them up to be warriors, to travel with other guards.

How many times had he told his sire that life

as a warrior, training other warriors, was not
for him? Yet his father chose to forget or ignore
his wishes, continuously pushing him onto the
training grounds. Insisting that he train the Grant
forces, fight every day. He believed it was Padraig's
duty as a Grant.

"Please reconsider, Padraig."

He'd walked out on those words. He'd tried
over and over to explain to his father why he felt
the need to leave, how he didn't enjoy fighting
like so many of his cousins. Most of the Ramsay
and Grant cousins were archers or swordsmen,
even the women. And he was no doubt skilled
with both weapons. But he didn't want the life of
a fighting man, and he didn't know how to make
his sire understand.

He hated this distance between them.

"Da, it just isn't the way I wish to spend my
life." He'd left, his mother's tears hurting him
more with each step he took, but he had to find
his own way.

How he wished he knew exactly what that
might be.

He wished to travel, see all the land, visit all his
cousins and friends. He had a vivid recollection of
the first time he'd ever been to Black Isle several
years ago and seen the beautiful countryside, rich
with forests, the quiet call of birdsong refreshing
his soul, blue sky over the mountains pulsing its
freshness through his blood.

Now he had cousins in Edinburgh, in the
Western Highlands, near East Lothian, Crieff,
Perth, any number of places he could visit and be

welcome, but he needed a purpose. He'd come to Black Isle because he'd heard of the trouble his cousins were having, and he'd been a help.

But what the hell was he to do now? Just leave?

A knock sounded on his door. Who on earth would come to find him in the middle of the night? He crossed the space and opened it a crack, then stepped back in surprise.

"Gisela, is something wrong?"

"Aye, I need you." She stepped into the darkness and closed the door behind her, setting the small candle she carried on a nearby table. She cupped his face with both hands, and her lips found his in an assault that was ruthless and wonderful at the same time. Their tongues dueled in a fierce mating, and he growled, lifting her in his arms and cupping her soft bottom, wishing to bury himself deep inside her. Only the thought of her brothers and his uncle kept him from following through.

She ran her hands down his arms, squeezing his hard muscles as he kissed her neck, teasing her ear lobe.

"Lass, you're driving me daft with desire. I want you like no other, but we cannot do this. I'll not defile you." The words came out, but now he had to make his traitorous member understand them.

She took only a single step away from him, panting. "Padraig, I'm no maiden. I was not going to save my virginity for that beast, so I gave it away to a man of my choice not long ago."

"Who?" A sudden jealousy burned through him. He forced himself to tamp it down, even as his hands still roamed over her luscious curves. Then he stopped to address his error. "'Tis none of my concern, lass, unless you've promised yourself to him. Forgive me, but 'twas an instantaneous reaction." He had no more right to inquire about her lovers than she did about his.

"It does not matter. He's dead from the curse. It was not for love, anyway. I was determined to give it to someone I trusted. But I wanted you to know that you'll not be defiling me." Her mouth met his again, and she parted her lips, angling them against his.

He let her have her way with him, savoring and enjoying every taste of her, every sensation she sent raging through him with a fire that would not abate. Gisela dropped her flimsy night rail and shift to the floor, baring her beauty to him. He had to stop kissing her to admire her gorgeous body, his mouth finding one nipple, then the other. She moaned, grabbing at his plaid and dropping it to the floor so he stood only in his tunic.

With a smile he removed it and settled her on his bed, pulling the covers back to give her a sense of decency, though he wasn't quite sure this lass cared. Lost in her passion, she said, "In me. Please, Padraig, I need you inside me."

He lay down next to her, drinking in her beauty with his eyes, then running his finger down the curve of her shoulder, down to the pulse that quickened on her wrist. He leaned down to kiss that sweet spot, and she moaned, "Padraig, please."

"Ah, lass, no need to rush this. Allow me the

chance to enjoy your beauty, your passion. You respond to me like no other." He moved his hand to her belly, causing her to gasp and jump at his touch. "'Tis just your belly," he said with a sly smirk.

Her hands moved to his shoulders while he drew a line across her abdomen, then up over her ribs until he cupped the mound of one breast, kneading it slowly in his hand. His thumb brushed across the peak of her nipple, and she whimpered, her gaze locked on his.

How had he been lucky enough to find a lass so responsive, so full of emotion and passion at his touch? "I could watch your passion all night, Gisela."

"Please, Padraig, you are torturing me."

"Be patient." He moved his hand across to the other breast, teased her a bit before running down the line in the center of her body, down her hips until he met the juncture of her thighs. Her legs jerked in response, and he decided to end his teasing and give her what she needed. His fingers found her folds, and he plunged one inside her slickness. Ah, she was so very ready for him! All he had to do was lift himself up, settle between her thighs, and push inside her.

But he just couldn't do it. "Lass, whether you have your maidenhead or not, if I do this, we'll marry. Are you ready to accept that?"

"Nay, just finish this. I beg you." She gripped his upper arms, her pelvis rocking against him, her back arching with need.

She was ready, he was ready. But he couldn't

do it.

"Padraig!"

His thumb found her nub while his fingers pumped inside her, and she went over the edge, climaxing with such a glorious look on her face that he was spellbound. Then, to his surprise, her hand found his shaft and cradled and squeezed him with her own magic ministrations, finishing him in a delicious release. How could it possibly be any better between them?

But he knew it would be someday.

"Why didn't you fill me, Padraig? I needed you."

"Because you wouldn't promise yourself to me. I admire you too much to take you in that way without an understanding between us. You are a noblewoman. I'll not truly bed you until you agree to be mine." He paused, then added, "Forever."

"I have too much to resolve in my life now. I cannot think on it. Give me time. Please."

"I will do that." It was best not to push her. She had indeed had too much happen in her life of late.

They lay in each other's arms for another hour, saying little until she finally broached the subject on both of their minds. "Padraig, you must leave. Please, do it for me. I fear for your life."

He kissed her forehead. "Gisela, Grant men don't answer to bullies. He doesn't frighten me. But if my presence ever puts you at risk, then I'll take my leave." He gazed into her eyes, surprised to see the sheen of tears there. "Don't cry. You are free of him."

"But I wish to be free to do as we wish."

"Would you like to marry me? I'm sure we would be verra happy together."

"Nay, I've already told you I won't," she said, pushing against his chest and pulling on a chest hair. "I'll not marry someone to free myself from that bastard. Escape isn't the right reason to marry." She tugged hard and ripped one hair, her gaze jumping to his to see his reaction.

"Ow, leave my chest hairs be, if you please."

She grinned, then licked his nipple and ran her teeth across the taut peak.

"Nay, no more. Before we get caught. I'll be one man against three brothers, and I'm not interested in that kind of a confrontation. I'm on your brother's land."

"But I came to you." She pulled on another chest hair before her hand moved over to fondle his nipple again.

He pulled away a wee bit, needing the distance to resist her better. He sat up, pulling her up next to him before he climbed out of bed to grab their clothing. He helped her dress before he donned his plaid.

"Padraig, I wish for you and me to have the time to explore each other, go on walks and boat rides, play with the bairns together. Travel the Highlands and the Lowlands. I'd love to meet your father and mother, your siblings. 'Tis what should be done when two people consider marriage. 'Tis what I want between us."

They finished dressing, and she leaned against

him, resting her head on his chest. "I wish for the time to listen to the beat of your heart, so I know when you're excited and when you're upset just by the change in rhythm. I don't wish to marry a man I don't know. I wish to know a man's true heart before we marry."

"I understand. One step at a time. We must let Donald forget you first." He escorted her to the door and reached for her candle, handing it to her. "Shall I walk you back to the keep?"

"Nay, I don't wish Torcall to see us together. He's on guard duty. I can sneak in the side door that's just a few steps away."

"I'm glad you came, lass," he whispered against her ear lobe.

She sighed before she kissed him goodbye. "I have so much hope for us."

"I do as well." He watched her until she was safely inside the keep. Then he leaned against his door frame, a strange sense of foreboding overtaking him.

He had a feeling they were going to need much more than hope to see this relationship through.

A wolf howled not far away, and he couldn't stop the shiver that coursed through him.

What would Donald MacKinnie do next?

CHAPTER FIVE

———————◆———————

GISELA SIGHED WHEN she climbed out of bed the next morning. She'd slept late because of her midnight interlude with Padraig. Every kiss, every touch was fresh in her mind.

If a life of marriage to Padraig Grant would be lying in his arms every night, perhaps she should reconsider his offer. As quickly as the idea formed in her mind, she dismissed it. She knew their current plan was the wise one. They had to wait for Donald to get over the cancellation of the betrothal, and who knew how long that would take.

She finished her ablutions and dressed with care, knowing she'd be seeing Padraig. She wished to look her best for him. Heading down the passageway, she had a sudden appreciation for Brigid and the way she had accepted being a mother to Tiernay and Kara. Brigid would have fed and dressed the two bairns this morn in her absence. In earlier days, it would have been Nonie who would have stepped in, but Gisela had little doubt that Brigid had taken complete care of the two wee ones, probably with Tara's help.

As she descended the staircase, she noticed things were not as they should be, the tone in the great hall one of seriousness and worry. The bairns were the only ones acting as if nothing unusual had happened, but the others showed their concern in their actions. Brigid had no smile on her face, Nonie continued to clean the same table over and over again, while Thebe casually made her way over to the healing chamber and leaned her ear against the closed door.

Something had indeed happened. And she guessed it had something to do with Donald MacKinnie.

Hell, but Donald was never one to wait patiently. Why would this be any different?

Brigid sat with the two wee ones near the hearth of the great hall, Kara galloping a little straw-stuffed fabric horse across the floor and Tiernay playing with blocks of wood, enjoying the sound of them clattering down as much as the process of stacking them up. Despite the bairns' happy play, Brigid ignored them, often staring into the flames of the hearth, the one true indication that something had gone wrong.

"What's wrong?" Gisela asked, her head scanning the hall for any indication of something awry. Thebe quickly rushed back to cleaning tables, her gaze returning again and again to the healing chamber at the end of the hall.

Nonie flitted back and forth. "You'll finish and get up to the bedchambers, Thebe. There'll be no hanging in the hall."

Thebe whirled around. "But I wish to see how

she is. Please, Nonie?"

"Nay, you'll not hear until midday anyway, the shape that poor lass was in. Finish that table and get upstairs with you. I'll be in the laird's chamber waiting for you." Nonie fetched a basket of clean linens and headed up the stairs.

Gisela was stuck on the phrase she'd heard— *shape that poor lass was in*. What lass? What had happened? She stared at the healing chamber herself, wishing its door would open and she'd learn more, but she'd have to get her information from Brigid. She moved to the hearth but didn't say anything right away. She would wait until Thebe had gone up the stairway.

The lass stopped at the top of the stairs and stared at the two of them before she moved on with a loud sigh.

Brigid tipped her head, indicating she wished for Gisela to move closer before she spoke. Thebe was probably hanging just around the corner to eavesdrop, but Gisela could not wait any longer to find out what was going on.

She pulled a chair close to Brigid's and gripped her arm. "What is it? Please tell me, Brigid. This is scaring me."

Brigid wouldn't look her in the eye, instead focusing on the bairns. "A woman was found in the woods early this morn. She'd been badly beaten. Torcall and Alvery brought her in to see if she could be saved."

"From here? Please say not from our clan." Her hand went to her throat as her mind flew to all the possible culprits for such an atrocious act, but only one name came to her mind.

Donald MacKinnie.

Just the thought of him sent her other hand into her hair, searching for a long section to twirl about her finger. The bastard.

"Not from here. Thebe said she could be from Clan Milton. 'Tis hard to tell when she was beaten so. Or she could have lived in one of the smaller villages just off the isle. No one knows yet. Jennet and Tara are with her now. They don't know if they can save her."

Gisela swallowed three times before she pushed herself to her feet and made her way to the door of the healing room. The bastard had truly earned his nickname of the Scourge of Black Isle, and he was continuing to live up to it.

The name had first arisen when Donald had visited her after the mystery of the curse had been solved. He'd come to pay his respects over the loss of her parents. The memory burned in her mind's eye.

He'd entered the hall with one guard behind him, ordering the man to stay by the door while he moved to where she sat by the hearth. In a most courteous way, he'd nodded to her and said kind words. "My sincerest condolences for the loss of your parents, Gisela. I understand this is a difficult time for you, but I wonder if you would honor me with a stroll out through the village."

"Nay, Donald. I don't feel like going out. I've just barely recovered myself, so I don't have the strength."

He pursed his lips and said, "I'm not asking. I'm

telling you we are to stroll together."

Stunned, she'd stared at him. "Nay." She'd looked around the hall, searching for her brothers, but none of them were there.

He'd grabbed her by the upper arm and yanked her to her feet. "We won't go far, but you will attend me. I've ordered you to do so."

Deciding perhaps it was best to go along with him since she had no one to assist her, she'd agreed, following him out the door, through the front gates, and into the village without saying another word. They'd passed Ethan in the courtyard, and she'd given him an imploring look, hoping he'd see she wished for help. But Ethan didn't always pick up on subtle clues, and that seemed to be the case that day. He didn't follow.

Once they were behind the castle at the edge of the village, she said, "Donald, being rude, abrupt, and hurting me will not convince me that our betrothal is something I still want. What say you if I change my mind?" Gisela's heart pounded at how roughly he'd handled her.

He grabbed her by both arms and pulled her closer, his eyes wide and his face in a reddened rage. "You will marry me, woman."

Stunned he'd ever address her so, she had no idea how to respond to him. This was not the man she'd known before the curse. Fortunately, Ethan had apparently gone to Shaw after all, who'd flown after them. He shouted when he caught sight of them.

"Set her down, you scourge!" Shaw had drawn his sword, and Donald had set her down immediately.

"I'll do as I wish with her. She's my betrothed." He'd said, shoving her behind his back.

"Nay, you'll not. She's my sister, and you'll not hurt her. Leave now. She's barely well enough to be up and about."

Then Marcas had arrived. "My guards will escort you off Matheson land, MacKinnie."

"I have a right to her. She's my betrothed."

"You lost that right when you mistreated her," Shaw declared. "Be gone."

That was the day she'd seen him kick a dog and strike his own mount before he left.

It had been Shaw that had pinned the word *scourge* on him, and it had stuck. He was indeed the Scourge of Black Isle, and he seemed to worsen with every passing day.

Brigid's voice brought her back to the present situation. Gisela found she was standing with her hand on the door latch for the healing room. "Gisela, don't go in. 'Tis a most unpleasant sight."

While she appreciated Brigid's thought, she also knew she couldn't ignore what had happened. She had to see for herself. She knocked softly and opened the door, then stepped inside. Jennet and Tara were tending a young woman, who lay on the bed limp as a fabric doll. Her cuts and bruises disguised her features—one eye had swollen shut, and a gash split her cheek. Her breathing was ragged and pained, telling Gisela much about the poor thing's condition.

Each touch of the linen square to the poor lass's beaten face brought a whimper, though Gisela guessed it was probably a good sign that she was awake and able to express herself. She didn't look like she'd live to see another morn.

"Has she said anything? A name? Anything?" Gisela whispered, leaning back against the door, afraid to step closer.

Tara glanced up. "Aye. Mayhap it would be better if you did not know."

"Did she say it was Donald?"

"Nay." Jennet turned to explain. "Just that it was a MacKinnie. She may not know Donald. He sent a message with her. If he hadn't had a purpose for her life, she'd probably be dead."

"The message?" She fisted her hands at her sides, fear edging up her back at what she was about to learn.

The woman's lips moved slowly as her leg shifted, perhaps in an effort to relieve her pain. "You're next."

Gisela's entire body went rigid. It felt as if Donald had taken possession of the lass and spoken through her lips. She stumbled to a stool and sat down, afraid she'd fall. She was still trying to process the threat when the door opened and Marcas stepped inside.

"How bad, Jennet?" he asked. "Will she live?" He moved over to stand closer to the lass, seeing her condition for himself.

"I think she will, though 'twill be days before we can send her home."

"Where is home?"

The woman moaned, but shook her head. "I lived in a small village just off the isle." Her bloodied, swollen lips moved with effort, but they worked. "Water, please?"

Tara helped her sit up and gave her a sip of water, though much of it drooled out of the corner of her mouth. "Please don't tell my da. He is still on Milton land. Not yet."

"What's your name?" Jennet asked.

"Dagga."

Marcas stepped forward so the lass could see him more easily. "Dagga, I'm the chieftain of Clan Matheson. You're with two of the finest healers in the Highlands. Who did this to you?"

Dagga's eyes opened wide, and she tried to shake her head, but she stilled, grimacing in pain and whimpering. "Nay, nay…kill me."

Tara shook her head at Marcas, indicating he shouldn't ask any more.

Dagga said, "Message. You're next."

"Me?" Marcas asked, his one word telling his feelings. "Why me?"

Dagga moaned, then whispered, "Nay, not you. Message is to a lass. She's next."

Gisela didn't want her brother to ask because she feared the answer. He did anyway. "Which lass?"

"Don't know. Don't remember." She did her best to push Marcas away.

Jennet said, "You should leave her for now. 'Tis obviously too frightening for her. Once she heals some, she may recall more."

"Has she said anything else to either of you? Torcall said she never spoke to them." He stepped away from the bed so he wouldn't upset the poor lass anymore. "This was done by a cruel bastard. I want his name."

Tara said, "You'll not get it this day. Mayhap on the morrow. She lived in a village off the isle."

Gisela couldn't move, so she was glad when Marcas took notice of her and ushered her out of the chamber and back into the hall. Padraig and Ethan stood there waiting for them. Ethan spoke first.

"Who did it?"

Marcas had his arm around her shoulders, and his strong care calmed her trembling. She couldn't even speak the necessary words. Brigid came up behind her husband.

"She won't say. She clearly fears retaliation. If she survives, we may learn more. But all we have is a message: 'You're next.' She doesn't recall who the message is meant for, and I'm not sure if she was given a name."

Padraig ran his hand across the scruff of his beard, pacing behind the group for a bit, then stopping to speak. "That bastard MacKinnie did it and is trying to frighten Gisela. This is all because she broke the betrothal."

Marcas let go of Gisela and stepped forward. "Lower your voice, Grant. I don't wish to share the information with everyone. You could be correct, or she could have remembered the wrong words. We have to wait until the morrow. Give her time to heal and hope we learn more."

Gisela looked to her brothers and Padraig. "It was Donald. I know it was."

"Aye, 'tis likely," Marcas said. "But we cannot

draw conclusions until we know for certain. There are other men out there who might hurt a woman. We'll just have to be patient. In the interim, I want all you women to stay inside the gates. No heading outside the curtain wall, even to the village, without an escort. Understood, Brigid? Please let your cousins know my feeling on this. I cannot worry about any of you." He pulled her close with an arm around her shoulders.

Brigid wrapped her arms around his waist and leaned into him. "We'll stay inside. I have no desire to step outside the gates, and I'll be sure to tell Jennet and Tara."

Marcas strode away after giving Brigid a quick kiss on the lips and Gisela a kiss on the forehead. "Ethan, come. We're going on patrol. There could be more."

They left Padraig with her, and she fell into his arms, grateful for his comfort. "Padraig, it must be him. What can we do? I cannot marry him, or I'll look the same every day, for the rest of my life."

Padraig led her over to the hearth, where Brigid had returned to the bairns. "Sit down, I'll get you some warm broth. You're shaking, Gisela."

Padraig headed toward the kitchen, and Gisela sat in silence, taking comfort from the children's happy chatter.

Padraig returned only a moment later, but still she startled. As she took a cup of broth off the tray Padraig bore, Brigid asked, "Did you learn anything at all about her attack?"

Gisela shared what the lass and Jennet and Tara had said. It was little enough.

"'Tis all you learned? Why did it happen?" Padraig persisted.

"Perhaps to send a message. And not only the words she was given."

"The message Marcas told of?" Padraig asked, his hands now fisted at his side.

Gisela took a deep swallow of the warm liquid he'd brought before she answered, strictly because she needed to stop the fine tremors all through her body. "Aye. 'You're next.'" She took another sip before lifting her gaze to Padraig and Brigid. She wanted to see if they would reach the same conclusion she had.

"Who's next?" Brigid asked.

"She didn't say, just that it was a lass. That was the message. Said she couldn't recall the name, if there was one." She stared into the flames of the fire crackling in the hearth. "The poor lass is in so much pain."

"Who do you think hurt her?" Brigid asked, glancing at Padraig.

"I'll tell you who it was," he said. "Donald, and the message is for Gisela. Someone needs to have a chat with that cruel bastard. This was what he meant by his threat to 'taunt' me."

"You mustn't confront him, Padraig. We don't know for sure it was him. If I know Donald, even if he didn't do it, he'll gladly claim it, if he thinks my fear will force me back to his side. He loves to frighten people. He'll slay you without a second thought merely for the fact you're a Grant. He has no fear, even of Grant warriors."

"Would he fear five hundred Grant warriors

coming to hunt him down?"

"Probably not. He's the type to believe in a hero's death. The only way to die is in battle, which is likely why he stayed away during the curse. 'Twould be a sin to die from sickness."

"Even so, someone needs to have a serious conversation with that man and his sire."

"Marcas and Shaw already tried," Brigid said. "Were you not there?"

"I was, but there were no threats from Clan Matheson. They broke the betrothal and left."

"Then mayhap Marcas will send a messenger confirming the betrothal is canceled."

"Or something better," Padraig muttered.

"Such as?" Gisela asked, afraid to hear his answer.

"Mayhap I'll have a conversation with the bastard myself. Let him know his actions have consequences."

Brigid arched a brow at Padraig. "Be careful committing Matheson warriors we don't have to a fight, Padraig."

"I'm not speaking of your warriors. I'd be warning him that I'll bring a full force of Grant warriors down on him if the attacks continue. Mayhap that he will take serious." Padraig's normally smiling face had changed to one of hate and a fury Gisela hadn't seen before. But even with that harsh look in his gaze, she knew he would never hurt her, never strike her or grab her the way Donald did. Padraig was an honorable man who knew how to control his temper.

Gisela stared at him when the meaning of

what he said dawned on her, that doing what he said could incite a clan war. Would he be able to mobilize that many warriors quickly? And she hated the thought of Padraig in harm's way. "Please be careful."

"I've had enough of his bloated view of his abilities. I'll put an end to it."

"Padraig, nay."

"Aye, Gisela. I'm done standing by. 'Tis time for action."

CHAPTER SIX

———◆———

PADRAIG AND SHAW left the next morn for MacKinnie land, Padraig anxious to put an end to this travesty that continued to plague Gisela in the form of Donald MacKinnie.

"I had hoped if we waited a bit longer, Dagga could have been more exact in her identification of her attacker," he said. "It would be good to have her word that the rumors about him are true."

"I want her to say it was Donald as much as you, but I don't know if she ever will. The poor lass is too frightened," Shaw said.

"'Struth is she may not know his name. He may not have told her. Not like he would tell his victim his name. He might hide his identity from her."

Shaw's gaze narrowed. "Most around here know Donald MacKinnie by sight. But perhaps he disguised himself. Or she's from the village and honestly doesn't know him. If so, she'll never name him."

"He's vain enough to declare his identity, so I had hoped she'd come out and tell us his name."

"He is vain enough, but not foolish enough. If you noticed the other day, Donald still fears his sire."

"'Twas an odd fear, was it not? Did the old man really mean he'd take a whip to his own son?"

Shaw stared straight ahead, his voice coming out in an eerie tone, the kind one would never question for its sincerity. "He would. Dougal and I were friends at one time. The old man can be a cruel bastard."

"At one time?" Shaw's whole countenance changed once he mentioned Dougal's name, becoming stiff, a deliberate mask of indifference. Still, Padraig persisted—maybe the connection would give them a way to end this mess without any more violence. "When?"

"Many years ago, but it means naught. *He* means naught to me now. We don't speak." Padraig opened his mouth to speak again, but Shaw turned his head to stare at him. "Leave it be. I'll speak no more on Dougal. Nothing I know of him will help us now."

He had to respect Shaw's wishes, so he curtailed his many questions.

Padraig and Shaw pulled their horses to a stop in front of the gates of Clan MacKinnie and were greeted by the same guard.

"State your purpose."

"I will speak with Donald MacKinnie. The name is Grant. Padraig Grant."

The guard must have recognized the name, because he climbed down quickly and ran straight for the keep. Padraig dismounted and turned to Shaw. "I just need you to stand beside me so I don't do anything foolish. I can have a fast temper, and if he slanders Gisela, I might lose it and go after him. It would be foolish to attack Donald in the middle of MacKinnie hall."

"Aye. I might be taking you back to Grant land in pieces. Mind your tongue and give him no excuse to challenge you. There is no honor in Donald's character at all. His sire has some, despite his cruelty, but Donald has none."

Padraig couldn't bear to watch Gisela suffer any longer. She was good at hiding her true feelings, but he'd learned to watch the kneading of her hands, the twisting and twirling of her hair, the amount of time she spent watching the door to the great hall. All revealed the amount of tension going through her.

He would put an end to it if there were any way possible. This was the best route, in his mind. Shaw dismounted and paced while they waited. The tension caused by one man could hardly be believed.

It wasn't long until they were ushered inside, the stable lads taking their horses. No one said anything as they made their way through the great hall and to the laird's solar, the same place they'd met before.

Donald was nowhere in sight, The chief spoke without inviting them to sit. "Ah, you've finally come to your senses and will approve the wedding, Shaw? Do you speak for your chief and your sister?"

Padraig cut him off by taking a step forward.

"Nay, I'm the one who called this meeting. I asked to speak with Donald. He needs to make amends for what he's done and not be allowed to continue."

"And just what is it you think Donald has done?"

Shaw stepped up beside Padraig and said, "A woman was found at the edge of our land early this morn. She was terribly beaten and said a MacKinnie beat her, though she knew not which one. She was quite clear that she was given a message and that this message was the reason she'd been beaten and left for our men to find. The message she was bade to give us was a threat against a woman within the Matheson clan."

The chieftain ran his hand down over his face, no emotion showing at all, then stared at his hands in his lap. The old man's face was lined with age and cracked with indifference. Even though his hair was still thick, his eyes, barely visible within the hardened sockets, glimmered with a sadness—a dramatic change since their last visit. When he lifted his face, a different expression was there, one Padraig hadn't seen before—a look of resignation.

Padraig pushed for more information. "Where is Donald? I need to speak with him. He's made a threat against Clan Matheson, and I believe 'tis because of me. He needs to answer for it."

The chieftain rubbed his hand across his rough beard. His voice was barely more than a whisper. The sound came out as an echo in the room that would last long after he'd spoken. "We haven't seen Donald since our last meeting, when Marcas canceled the betrothal. He disappeared and has not returned. If I'd have known, I'd have stopped him from leaving. I know not what else to say but that he's changed. He's not the same son I've known for years."

Shaw leaned across the table toward the chieftain. "Then he could be on a killing spree, MacKinnie. You must stop him."

He kept his gaze on Shaw, ignoring Padraig. "I have no idea where he is. I've never known him to be gone this long, and you can trust that he's going to see it through, whatever he has planned. We argued, and I need not tell you what about. He didn't like what I had to say—that I wouldn't attack your clan in order to force Gisela to wed him—so he left, as angry as ever I've seen him. Donald can be quite belligerent. More and more over the last year."

Shaw paced the chamber. "He nearly killed a poor lass, one from a village just off the isle, so you'll be hearing about that, MacKinnie."

"How do you know it was him? Did she identify Donald specifically?" The old man leaned back in his chair, the fight back in his eyes.

"Nay," Shaw answered. "But she did identify the man who attacked her as a MacKinnie. She's scared to say any more, and I cannot fault her for that. When we found her, she was close to death. It takes a cruel man to inflict those kinds of bruises on an innocent lass."

"I don't believe it was Donald. He's after Grant, not some odd lass he found."

"We've no proof it was Donald, but either way, you need to find your son and if it wasn't him, the clan member who committed the crime," Padraig said. "The woman's attacker left a message for a female in our clan saying she would be next. That has to be a threat against Gisela."

The old man bolted so quickly to his feet that he nearly fell over. "My son would not hurt Gisela. He's in love with her and has been for a long time. That tells me it was *not* Donald. Take your leave now, and take your nasty lies and accusations with you."

"You know a sheriff would view Donald as a suspect. I suggest you find out what is happening among the men in your clan. Mayhap you need to send your own patrol out for Donald, if he's as stubborn as you say. How many lasses will he harm? How many will he kill?" Shaw pinned Fearchar MacKinnie with a look. "If he touches my sister, I'll kill him with my bare hands."

Padraig added his own voice. "And I'll cut his body up and roast it over the fire. Tell us where we can find him. I know you have some ideas." Padraig set his hands on his hips, waiting for an answer.

"My son did not beat that woman, whoever she was. I want her name."

"We'll not share that information, Chief." Padraig took a step closer to him, moving his hand to the hilt of his sword.

"Take your hand off your weapon, Grant. I have plenty of warriors who will cut your throat if you attack me." He ran his hands through his hair again, closing his eyes. "I disagree with what you say. Even though I believe Donald has changed, he won't harm Gisela. In his own twisted mind, he adores her."

"Then who is he after?" Shaw demanded.

The old chieftain pointed a finger at Padraig Grant. "He thinks this is all your fault, Grant. He'll make you pay, one way or the other. I know my son. By some sly attack, he'll see you suffer and likely dead. He believes if you're gone, all will be well. He has no reason to harm an innocent lass."

"So we're to just ignore the hurt that's been done to this lass sheltering in our home and not search out Donald on your say so? How will the next message come, I wonder—on a beaten child's tongue? 'Tis a most ridiculous position, MacKinnie."

"There's only one solution," the chief said. "Though you'll not like it.

Padraig snorted. "I know a solution, and I'd be glad to oblige you—find your son and kill him. That will put an end to Gisela's fear and protect all the lasses."

"No need to do that," MacKinnie said. "He's my son, and I'll defend his life to the last."

"I don't see any other way," Padraig said, his lips pursed flat. He did his best to contain his anger, but holding it back was proving a greater challenge than most he'd faced.

"What's your solution then, MacKinnie?" Shaw asked.

"Go home, Grant. If you're no longer on Black Isle, he'll not see you as a rival."

"Except that won't satisfy him, because Gisela will still refuse to marry him," Shaw said. "And even if she conceded to the marriage to save others from harm, none of her family would allow it, especially after seeing the damage he did to the lass found in the forest. You may not believe he's capable, but I do. He needs to be stopped, and he won't stop until Gisela gives herself to him."

"Do as you wish, then. I'm tired. You may take your leave. If you're wise, Grant, you'll go home and leave Black Isle in peace. Ever since the Ramsays and Grants came to our beloved land, we've had naught but trouble. Think you 'tis because of us? I don't. I know the guilty parties." His finger came up and pointed at Padraig.

Padraig stared long and hard at the chieftain. His departure seemed like an easy enough solution, but what would happen to Gisela? He didn't like anything about the situation, nor did he trust this chieftain.

As if reading his mind, the chief's voice came out in a hoarse gasp. "I think Donald could accept Gisela not marrying him, but not if he thinks she's marrying another. He has his pride, Shaw. Mayhap your clan could consider the embarrassment you've caused him and come up with a solution to make amends."

"Why should we?" Shaw asked, clearly exasperated. "I don't see any other solution other than to involve the sheriff, and I'm not opposed to doing that."

"Because if you don't try to rectify the situation you started, Donald will. He believes he's been wronged, and you won't like the way he chooses to set the situation to rights."

Padraig glanced at Shaw, who said, "We've had our say. We'll take our leave and search for the bastard all the way home."

Padraig nodded, and he and Shaw stalked out of the room. The only thought that crossed his mind was whether or not the old man was right.

If he left Black Isle, would Gisela be safe from Donald? Or would that put her in more danger?

He had some thinking to do.

——— ◆ ———

Gisela hesitated outside the door to the healing chamber, wishing to talk to Dagga but afraid of what she might learn. Had her former betrothed beaten an innocent lass because Gisela had changed her mind about their betrothal? Was she at fault for all Dagga had suffered?

She opened the door, peering around the edge of it before stepping inside. The poor lass's expression was one of fear, her gaze darting back and forth from the door to the other side of the chamber as if she were a cornered animal, waiting to be snapped up by a beast's jaws.

Was Donald the beast she feared?

Someone entered behind her and gripped her shoulders. She started, looking back to see who had approached her. Tara stood there, nodding her encouragement to move forward. "'Tis time for you to find out the truth."

Glancing beyond Tara, she caught Nonie's gaze on her as she cleaned one of the tables, the pity evident on her face, even across such a distance.

She vowed to not be deterred from her mission and propelled herself forward until she stood next to the lass's bed.

Up close, her appearance was far worse. One eye was still swollen shut while the other followed her movement much as she used to track a wasp, for fear of being stung. Dagga's one visible hand gripped the coverlet as if it were a weapon she could swing at an interloper, but she never moved it, the white of her knuckles never relenting to pink.

Her skin was covered in mottled bruises of purple, blue, yellow—her arms, legs, face, everywhere Gisela could see. Cuts dotted her arm, and now that she was this close, she could make out a distinct handprint on Dagga's cheek. Donald had slapped her hard. Tara or Jennet had neatly stitched the gash on her other cheek.

"May I sit, Dagga?" she asked, reaching for a nearby stool when the woman nodded her agreement.

"What do you want? I've answered many questions already," Dagga asked.

Gisela wasn't quite sure how to answer her. Thankfully, Tara spoke first.

"This is Gisela, the Matheson chieftain's sister. 'Tis important for us to know who attacked you and what kind of threat they might be to others. Do you know his name?"

Dagga shook her head. "I've said nay already."

"Can you describe him for us?" Tara's tone was so gentle, Dagga was softening to their inquisition.

She whispered, her good eye darting around the room, as if fearing the wrong person would overhear. "He was a large man, fair-haired, handsome, and he wore a MacKinnie plaid."

Tara glanced at Gisela. Her eyes threatened to mist up at this revelation, but she managed to curb her response.

"You delivered his message, that someone here is 'next,' but do you have any other clues about why he hurt you or who the message was for? Is he angry with me?" Gisela asked, afraid to hear her answer.

Dagga frowned, then leaned her head back against the pillow to stare up at the ceiling. She hesitated, her fingers going up to lightly touch her bruised lips. When she finally lifted her head and spoke, her words weren't what Gisela expected at all.

"He's not upset with you. But I do recall another thing he said."

"What?" Gisela folded her hands together on her lap, wondering if she would draw blood, her nails bit into her palms so.

"He's angry with another man." Dagga paused again, closing her eyes for a moment. Then her eyes flew open, a look of satisfaction crossing her face. "Aye, a Grant warrior. He said the Grant warrior must go home."

Gisela couldn't stop her hands from trembling. She bolted up from the stool and strode away, turning her back to Dagga. Tara stepped forward, taking over the conversation and allowing Gisela the space to step away and gather herself.

Gisela heard the scrape of the stool as Tara sat. "Did he say which Grant warrior? My mother is from Clan Grant, and there are many Grant warriors. It would help if we knew which one. Take your time and think on it, Dagga. You are being verra helpful to us. If there is anything I can do to make you more comfortable, please say so."

Gisela stood in a shadow near the door. The fire in the hearth was down to burning embers, and the lack of light allowed her to hide for a moment. She wanted to keep speaking with Dagga, but she couldn't hide her concern over this revelation and the threat aimed at Padraig. She had to regain control of her frazzled emotions before she went back to the wounded lass.

"He didn't mention a name. But when he started striking me," Dagga said, her voice now shaking, "he said he'd fix that Grant warrior for taking his lass from him. I'm sorry, but I cannot…"

Tara patted her arm and brought the coverlet up to her chin. "Hush. 'Tis enough. You've been most helpful, Dagga. My thanks to you."

"Please don't send me home alone. I fear he'll find me."

Gisela stepped forward. "You may stay as long as you need, and we'll contact whomever you like. And when you are ready to return home, we'll send guards along to protect you. Do not worry yourself on it."

Dagga rolled onto her side away from them, then Tara held her finger to her lips to indicate that Gisela shouldn't speak again.

She nodded, out of words in any case. Gisela's

eyes locked on Tara's as she crossed to the door. Tara linked her arm with hers comfortingly as she led her out of the chamber.

Once in the hall, Gisela hurried to a chair in front of the hearth, tears falling from her eyes. Brigid entered from abovestairs, Jennet behind her.

"What's wrong?" Jennet called out.

Tara said, "We just discovered that Donald is not out to get Gisela but instead wishes to be rid of Padraig. He wants the Grant warrior who stole his lass."

"What will we do?" Gisela asked, knowing the answer but not considering it because she didn't wish it to be the only path forward.

Jennet shrugged, glanced at her two cousins, and announced, "'Tis a simple situation. Padraig must leave. Then Donald should stop his attacks."

Brigid said, "Somehow, I don't think 'twill be so easy. I'm anxious to hear what Padraig learns at Clan MacKinnie."

Marcas entered through the front door halfway through her sentence. "What don't you think will be easy? It sounds like you've learned something more." He sidled over to his wife and wrapped his arms around her from behind, nuzzling her neck. "Just the important information."

"If you wish to hear my answer, husband, you'll not distract me so," she answered, sighing at his attentions.

Jennet rolled her eyes at the two lovers, who still carried on as if they'd just met.

Tara explained. "Dagga said Donald promised

to 'fix' the Grant warrior who stole his lass. That would be Padraig. We think he must leave immediately."

"Not necessarily," Marcas replied.

"I agree," Jennet said. "Padraig leaving may not be the best solution."

Ethan entered from the kitchens and moved over next to Jennet, wrapping his arm around her waist while she spoke. "I agree with you, Jennet."

Gisela fell into a chair with a huff. "I'm confused. Please explain, Ethan."

Ethan looked to Jennet, but she nodded to him to continue. "Men like Donald are looking for any reason to cause trouble. Attacking the lass was meant as a scare tactic, but it's just the beginning. Padraig gave him a reason to act, but if Padraig leaves, it won't take Donald long to find another offense he feels he has to right, and he'll start up again. His father has always had to control him. Let us hope he continues to do so."

Padraig came in through the door, Shaw directly behind him. "Not this time," the youngest Matheson brother said.

Gisela rushed to Padraig, meeting him halfway across the room. "Padraig, I don't understand what he means. I think you must leave or you'll not be safe."

Padraig took her hand and ushered her back over to a chair to sit. "I suspect it will not matter if I go or stay."

"What did you learn?" Marcas asked, running his hand up and down Brigid's arm in a light caress.

Padraig sighed, then squared his shoulders. "Donald departed the castle after we left and hasn't returned. His sire doesn't know where he is. But he definitely is after me, not you, Gisela. And his father agrees that Donald has changed, like you've said. He's not the same man he used to be, though he doesn't know the cause. And who knows what that means for our decisions now. He's completely uncontrolled."

"What the hell?" Marcas asked. "Donald has never left Black Isle, as far as I know. He's always been loyal to his sire. Why would he abandon MacKinnie lands?"

"I'm not sure. We couldn't come up with any ideas. We tried to ask some of the stable lads as we were leaving, but no one said anything. They were all as surprised as we were. But I fear what it means."

Gisela's heartbeat quickened, her palms grew slick with sweat, and the pain in her head throbbed at an alarming rate. She had no idea what to make of all this news. Everything in her life had gone from steady improvement to chaos and confusion, from hope to dread.

But Donald leaving home? She had a thought and hated the flare of relief she'd feel if she were right. "Do you think it could be possible that Donald is dead, and that's why he's not returned?"

"Nay," Marcas answered. "We have Dagga as witness that he's still living. I believe there is only one likely explanation."

"What?" she asked, twisting her gown into a wrinkled mess.

"Donald is on the hunt, on a rampage to prove himself stronger and more powerful than Padraig. There will be no stopping him."

"But we must stop him, Marcas. Somehow. I fear for all of us, and this is all my fault."

Padraig growled and he ran his hands through his long locks before he calmed and faced her. "None of this is your fault, Gisela. 'Tis all the MacKinnies who are at fault. But there is a solution. And I think 'tis the only possible solution. The only way to stop him."

Everyone spoke at once, asking what he meant. But Gisela held very still, almost afraid of his answer, knowing whatever it was would put someone at greater risk than ever. Probably Padraig.

Padraig held his arms up to quiet everyone. Then he turned to her. "There is only one way to stop him, and we must do it as soon as possible."

"For Heaven's sake, what?" Brigid yelled.

He turned to Gisela and said, "Marry me. We'll marry and go far away. Say you will, Gisela."

She only had one word in her mind, but he wouldn't like it. He wouldn't understand, so she didn't try to explain. But she knew that if they married, Donald would get worse, and people would suffer on her account. If they left, he would go after her family, and he would target those she loved more than any of the others: Kara and Tiernay.

She couldn't risk his hurting the two bairns.

"Gisela Matheson, will you marry me?" Padraig asked.

"Nay, Padraig Grant. I cannot." She raced up the staircase to hide her tears.

CHAPTER SEVEN

———————◆———————

PADRAIG COULDN'T MOVE. Marcas and Brigid chased Gisela, and the others moved around the hall in a flurry. But his feet felt anchored to the floor. Had he truly just proposed to her?

Had she truly just turned him down?

He fell into the closest chair, not knowing what to do next. Should he go after her? Leave her for a bit and talk to her later?

Or perhaps it was time to take his leave, relieve the troubles for the Mathesons, give in to Donald's demands. Perhaps if he left, the bastard would truly leave Gisela and the other lasses alone.

If there was even a chance he would stop his rampage, then it was the right thing to do. Especially after he'd asked the lass he loved to marry him and she'd turned him down.

Love? Did he love Gisela? He didn't know his own mind, his own heart. He adored spending time with her. Their passion was the same, their laughter was special, and they shared a unique sense of humor.

But that didn't mean they should marry. Their

relationship was too new. He was a fool to have proposed, so he thought it best to let her go.

He bent down and picked up Tiernay, who was busy chewing on something. Brigid or one of the others would return soon to mind the bairns, but until then, they could distract him from his swirling thoughts. Kara looked up at him as if waiting for him to make an announcement. He would have to find some way to occupy the wee ones.

"Close your eyes, Kara. Tiernay and I will hide, then you have to find us."

"I pwomise no' to peek," she said, covering her eyes with her hands.

Padraig moved over to the door and hid between two mantles hanging on pegs. He didn't care that his feet would stick out. A bairn Kara's age could take forever to find someone hidden, and he didn't wish to prolong the chase.

He covered their faces with the wool cloak, holding Tiernay on his hip. He whispered, "We're hiding. She'll not see us." The lad giggled, his eyes wide.

They stayed still when she shouted, "I'm coming for you."

Padraig knew the exact moment she saw them because she broke into a wild giggle and her feet quickened against the floor, heading straight for them. When she was nearly upon them, he jumped out with a roar and both bairns erupted into giggles.

"Your turn, Kara. You hide now."

Kara moved over to the mantles and stood next

to one, closing her eyes. "You can't find me. I'm hiding."

That was new to him. He'd played with many cousins when he was younger, knowing their hiding spots were always easy, but this was different. If she closed her eyes, she thought she was hiding, apparently. Was that how this game would play?

"Where is Kara, Tiernay? I can't find her, can you?"

Kara giggled, and Tiernay quickly pointed to his sister. She didn't open her eyes, so Padraig had to guess she still thought she was invisible. "Where is Kara?"

Tiernay pointed, eagerly showing Padraig where his sister was hiding. As if she could see Tiernay, the lass giggled uncontrollably.

"I just don't see her anywhere," Padraig said, playing along. The fun distracted him from his failed marriage betrothal, and he embraced it.

A moment later, she opened her eyes and shouted, "Here I am!"

"We found her! Hide again, Kara."

Kara ran over to hide behind a chest, her feet sticking out.

"Where's Kara? I can't find her." He and Tiernay stomped around the hall until he came close to her, then he reached down and tickled her feet, eliciting giggles and wiggles galore. "I found two feet sticking out. I think we found your sister, Tiernay."

Kara came out of her spot, tears running down her face. "Nay, I had my eyes closed. You could not see me with my eyes closed. I was hiding."

Padraig didn't know what to say, so he set Tiernay down and reached for Kara. "I've found you now, you wee trickster." He tossed her up in the air until her giggles filled the hall again. When he finally set her down, her laughter stopped, and he heard sobbing coming from behind him.

He set Kara down next to Tiernay and turned around, surprised to see Gisela standing there, tears streaking her cheeks. "You are so wonderful with the bairns. You'll make someone a wonderful husband. But I love them too much to leave them. I cannot leave Matheson land. Before the curse, all I wished to do was leave. Now I wish to stay here forever, with those I love and almost lost. I fear if you and I left together, he might go after these two when he learned of it. I couldn't bear it. I'm so sorry, Padraig."

Padraig stepped over to engulf the sobbing woman in his arms. He held her close, and she cried into his shoulder, soaking his tunic with her tears. "Padraig, there is no one like you, but please do not be angry with me. 'Tis too soon for us. I must take care of my homeland, protect my niece and nephew, help my brother bring the clan back to what it was before the curse."

"I understand, lass. The clan is a strong pull for you. You must do what is in your heart. Do not apologize for turning me down. I recognize 'tis too early for us, and of course you cannot risk the bairns." He stood back and cupped her cheeks. "I cannot tell you your thinking is wrong. If he found out we left together, he would certainly try threats and violence to bring you back. We cannot risk it." He kissed her lips tenderly and whispered, "'Tis not our time, lass."

Kara pulled on Gisela's gown. "Why you crying, Auntie?"

Gisela bent down and picked up her niece, kissing her cheek. "Never fear, lassie. I stubbed my toe and it hurt, but I'm much better now."

"No mo' cwying?"

"No more crying. I'm done now." She gave her eyes one last swipe and leaned against Padraig and said, "I hope you'll forgive me."

"There is nothing to forgive. A marriage should be based on two people who love and cherish each other, who know each other well, so well that they know each other's thoughts. We are not so close yet. We have a wonderful start, but we have more to learn about each other. I should have thought through my suggestion and spoken to you about it in private." Still, it stung to have her reject him so quickly, so thoroughly.

Of course, he hadn't expected to propose marriage. It was all too unconventional, too new, too unpredictable.

Her rejection left him only one alternative to the chaos they were in.

He had to leave Matheson land, but instead of making it common knowledge to everyone, he'd have to decide who he would tell. He didn't wish to draw attention to the fact that he'd be on the road alone. While he wasn't afraid of Donald, he could see that the man was losing his ability to reason. Donald was proving to indeed be sneaky and sly.

Padraig was used to people coming directly at him.

He would go the next morn. There was no reason to wait.

———— ♦ ————

Gisela hurried around the chamber, grabbing her clothing and cleaning her mouth with a cloth. Dawn was no more than a rosy glow on the horizon, but Tara had come to her and told her Padraig was outside, waiting to speak with her and Marcas. She dressed quickly and hurried into the stables where Padraig awaited her.

When she arrived, he approached her, cupping her face and kissing her lightly on the lips. "I must go, Gisela. If there's the slightest chance it will help, I must try it. For you, for Clan Matheson, for all the lasses here on Black Isle."

Tears came quickly, filling her eyes and drenching her cheeks in seconds. "Padraig, nay." She buried her face in his shoulder and sobbed, unable to stop even though she knew he was doing the right thing.

Marcas and Tara came in from outside. Marcas said, "Grant, many thanks for your assistance during our difficulties. I'm sorry to lose you. Are you sure you don't wish to take a few guards with you?"

"Nay, you need them more than I do." His fingers had found their way to the nape of her neck, and he massaged her skin so masterfully she nearly moaned. "But if things worsen, send word and I'll return with a force of Grant warriors large enough to aid in whatever way you need. That's a promise, my friend."

"You're welcome here any time, with or without your warriors." Marcas clasped his shoulder as a sign of support and left them alone, Tara leaving with a quick nod.

"Take care, cousin."

Gisela leaned her head back and whispered, "I love you, Padraig. I'm just not ready…"

"And I love you, but please hush, lass." He set a finger to her lips. "I'm more interested in a wedding that could be filled with laughter instead of being rushed and full of fear. Our time will come." He kissed her on the lips again, then on her cheek and her forehead before stepping back. With a flourish, he quickly bent at the waist, his arm sweeping out in wide movement. "If you are ever in need of the finest man in all the land, just send a missive and I'll be here immediately."

She giggled, loving that handsome smile he always wore. "Godspeed, Padraig."

He left quickly, and Gisela felt like she'd lost her best friend. Marcas escorted her back to the hall where she sat and stared into her porridge for more than two hours. Her heart ached from knowing it would be a long time before she'd ever see Padraig Grant again, if ever. And she couldn't help that nagging feeling that perhaps she'd made a mistake turning him down.

Brigid sat across from her, setting down a bowl of porridge she'd retrieved from the kitchens. "I heard that Padraig took his leave."

"Aye," Gisela mumbled, not even trying to hide her heavy sigh. "I'll miss him terribly."

"We all will, but I think he made a wise decision. Donald must relent in his pursuit before Padraig can court you properly. You don't need Donald always bothering you, interfering with your relationship, and I don't believe he would have ever let up while Padraig was here as a rival. A year from now, he could be married to someone else, and he'll forget all about you."

"I hope you're right. My fear is he'll either follow Padraig or try to steal me away to marry him. I'm not sure which is more likely."

Brigid pursed her lips. "Those are two poor alternatives. I share your fear that Donald will try to steal you. He's impatient for his desires. You must be verra careful not to be caught outside the gates for at least two moons, mayhap longer. He'll forget you in time, move on to another lass who stirs his loins."

Gisela only arched her brow at that blunt pronouncement. She let out a small, unladylike snort. "Somehow, knowing I've stirred Donald's loins does not make me feel special."

Brigid grinned and wrinkled her nose at her. "You are deserving of someone much better than that big brute." Nonie came down the staircase, carrying the two bairns with her, one on each hip. Brigid hopped out of her chair. "Nonie, why did you not call me? I could have helped you with them."

"Nay, you have enough to do. I just gave them a quick tub bath because Tiernay made a mess."

Gisela reached for her nephew while Brigid lifted Kara from Nonie's capable arms. Gisela kissed his forehead and announced, "My nephew is quite sweet-smelling now."

"Miwk," Tiernay said, doing his best to pronounce his desired drink.

Thebe entered from the kitchens, bringing a fresh pitcher of goat's milk for the bairns. "Here you all go, nice and fresh. And I have a tray of baked apples with some bread just out of the ovens."

Kara clapped with delight as she sat at the table, a pillow boosting her to the right height. All was quiet for a few moments as everyone chose the food they wanted and began to fill their bellies. Thebe came over next to Gisela and whispered, "I heard Donald is coming to visit this morn."

Gisela stared at the servant. "How do you know this?"

"I heard when I went home last eve to see Mama. Someone told me." Thebe dropped her gaze as if feeling guilty for the news she brought.

"My thanks for the information, but we have not heard as such." She turned back around to her food, not wishing to give the wagging tongue anything more to talk about.

Gisela closed her eyes and said a quick prayer that he would stay away, but perhaps it would be best if they met one last time, just to make everything perfectly clear. If only he would listen to her. The only way such a conversation would happen would be if he came here. She was never going to his holding, that was certain.

The rest of the meal passed with just a few niceties exchanged between the adults and the chatter of the bairns. Gisela was too upset at the prospect of Donald returning to eat much. She focused on Kara and Tiernay, making sure they ate all they wished to have.

During the horrific period of waiting for the bastard to show up, she considered what she would say to him and how she would answer his demands. And he would have demands. She couldn't imagine the man saying anything kind, or even polite, to her.

She didn't have to wait long. About halfway through breakfast, Timm, Alvery's son who worked in the stable, hurried across the hall to her side. "Donald MacKinnie is here for you, my lady," he said, his eyes wide.

Marcas marched in behind Timm. "He'll see you here with me at your side, Gisela."

Shaw came in next, cursing and pacing.

Brigid stepped over to take the two bairns, handing Tiernay to Nonie. "Wait until you see what Jennet and I have abovestairs for you, Kara. We're going to play with some new toys."

Kara giggled and gladly gripped Brigid's shoulder as she lifted her onto her hip. Brigid climbed the stairs with Nonie and Tiernay behind her, Jennet at the rear.

As Tara moved closer to Gisela, offering her silent support, Ethan entered with Donald and his small group behind him. They carried no weapons—perhaps they'd been forced to lay them aside upon entry.

Marcas led Gisela over to the hearth, stopping in front of a chair, but she glared at her brother and said, "I cannot sit."

"Accepted, and I don't blame you," he whispered. "Stay next to me."

Donald strode across the space, a wide smile on his handsome face. If she didn't know what was actually behind those twinkling eyes, she might have been interested in him. Just as she had once been—before everything changed, including him. She waited and tried to remember to breathe.

"Fair Gisela," he said, half bowing to her. "I am pleased to see that you've acceded to my demands and sent the Grant warrior on his way. I have a priest awaiting our decision—will you marry me here this eve or on the morrow on MacKinnie land?"

Gisela did her best not to let her distaste show on her face. His words were as welcome as a steaming plate of horse droppings. Even though she'd more than half expected something like this, her cheeks flushed with anger at his presumption.

Marcas gripped her arm and gave her a look that said *I'll answer for you*. "Gisela will not be marrying you, Donald. I'll not allow it. I thought we'd made it clear when we stood in your hall that the betrothal was ended."

Donald snorted. "Ended for a short time only. The man who distracted her is gone now, so she can focus all her attention on me, as it should be. She'll come to MacKinnie Castle, learn what I wish her to do to please me, then marry me on the morrow. What you said was not accepted by my laird or by me. We are still betrothed, so I wish to put an end to this conflict and marry with haste. Can you not see that she is dishonoring you, Matheson? Tell your sister she was promised by your sire and you will honor that promise. If not now, then the morrow. I'll accept nothing less."

"Nay," Shaw said, "You daft bastard, she's not marrying you. You think we'll give you free rein to beat her to the size of a mouse like you did the lass in the forest? You're foolish if you do. Even your sire despairs for you. He said he had no idea where you'd gone, other than wrong in the head."

Gisela stilled as Donald's hands fisted at his sides, his face turning a deep red again as he took in Shaw's words. Though she was grateful the small group had been forced to leave their weapons outside the hall, she still kept an eye on his hands. Hands that were as capable of inflicting pain as any weapon. One of them moved to the side of his head and gripped his blond hair. The noise he made was neither moan nor growl, but something between the two and angry as a cornered boar. He lifted his gaze to her.

"Gisela, are you denying me? I wish to hear it from your lips." His voice had changed to a low monotone she didn't like at all. A low growl erupted from between his clenched teeth, telling her exactly how he felt.

"Donald, please. I'm not the same lass I was when we met. The curse has changed everything, including me, and we're not suited any longer." Her hands kneaded her skirt, though she wished she could hide any display of her distress.

Donald was not a stable man, and everyone knew it.

He moved so quickly that she couldn't dodge him. Grabbing her by both arms, he jerked her close and brought his teeth down on her neck below her ear, biting her hard. She cried out and kicked against his legs.

"Ow! Let me go!"

Marcas drew his sword, but Ethan was quicker. Coming up behind Donald, he put his dagger to the other man's throat. "I will use it. Do not doubt me. Let my sister go."

Donald released her with a shove and a grin. "I have branded you mine. You'll never marry another. I'll make it known that I have marked you, and anyone who dares to touch you will die at my hand."

Ethan took a half step back, just enough to let Donald move toward the door. "Leave and be glad you still have life. Never return."

Shaw kept the other members of Donald's retinue frozen in place with his sword. Marcas held his own blade ready, and though he appeared relaxed, Gisela knew he could strike quick as a snake. He gestured toward the door with the steel. "Get out, all of you. There is no betrothal, and Gisela will never marry you, MacKinnie. You'll never be allowed inside the gates of Eddirdale Castle again."

Donald stepped backward, still grinning. "We shall see." He made his way to the door, then turned.

"Go and say nothing, MacKinnie. I'm warning you," Shaw said.

"You're mine, Gisela. Forever." His finger came up and pointed directly at her. "Marked."

Gisela fell back and put her hand to her neck where he'd bitten her. When she drew it away, her fingers came away wet with her own blood.

He'd never leave her alone.

CHAPTER EIGHT

———————◆———————

A S PADRAIG CROSSED into Grant land two days after leaving Black Isle, he watched for the patrol he knew was always out, looking for reivers or anyone else foolish enough to visit Grant land with unsavory motives. Dusk was nearly upon him, though he'd hoped to get home ahead of the night, sleep in his own home this eve.

It wasn't long before he spotted them, and they him. A group of about a half dozen men on horseback approached, Jake in the lead.

"Greetings to you, cousin. Glad to have you back. Are you staying for a while, or are you going to continue your imitation of Uncle Logan and go wandering off again?" Jake asked, leaning to clasp hands with Padraig in greeting.

"I came from Black Isle, where I've been for a while, but I suspect you already know that."

Jake turned his horse to ride abreast with Padraig, making a sign to the rest of the group that they were to continue on their patrol. One other joined him, his son Alasdair, now eight winters old.

"You travel alone from Black Isle?" Jake asked with a sideways glance. "I understand why your mother gets upset over your choice of travel. 'Tis never good to travel alone. Even Uncle Logan travels with Aunt Gwyneth, who can defend herself from reivers as well as you or I."

"I'll not tell my mother I traveled alone unless she asks," Padraig replied, a small smile on his face.

"Your sire will know. The Grant elders know all."

"I'll handle my sire."

"I'll not mention it to anyone, though as laird and your cousin, I'll suggest you travel with no less than three men. 'Tis summer when reiving is at its best." The season for cattle stealing and bride stealing was indeed upon them. Jake glanced over his shoulder at his son, who nodded, apparently agreeing with the unspoken request to not speak of the issue. Alasdair was the most loyal of the three grandsons born the same day.

Padraig had no argument against Jake's advice, so said nothing. Why did he insist on traveling alone? He didn't spend much time thinking on it—perhaps he was too impulsive.

Padraig studied his cousin. "You look more and more like your sire every time I see you. And Alasdair looks like Grandda, too."

"Aye, so everyone says. Connor's the same, though a wee bit taller than me and Papa." He glanced over at his son. "Alasdair will be the same someday."

"I can already beat both my cousins in a fight, Alick and Els. I'm taller and stronger," Alasdair said. "I can use a real sword. I even picked up Grandda's the other day. I could only swing it two times, but I did." The pride the lad felt speaking of his grandfather, the renowned Alexander Grant, was evident in the glow of his eyes and the tone of his voice. Padraig's Uncle Alex was indeed a true wonder to watch in battle.

"I think your shoulders are broader, Jake. Surely you can take your father in the lists at this point." Padraig had watched Uncle Alex fight many times, astounded by the man's power and focus, even as he approached his sixth decade. He had silver streaks in his hair, but still won appreciative looks from women and warriors alike.

"I no longer try. Mayhap maturity gifted me with a wee bit of wisdom. I prefer to allow his reputation to stand. Connor or Loki will take his place someday, but Papa has earned his glory."

"And Alasdair will join Connor as one of the great Grant warriors, I think," Padraig said, peeking at his younger cousin, who was now puffed up with a bit of pride. But he knew there was one person who could unsettle the three cousins born on the same night. "And how about Dyna?"

Alasdair turned quite serious, not enjoying the topic. "We don't play games with Dyna. She fixes us if we do."

Dyna, the only girl among the four younger cousins who ran as a pack, had shown signs of being a seer before Padraig had left for Black Isle.

"Does she? Is she getting better at it or worsening?" Padraig asked, unable to stop the grin that crossed his face.

Poor Alasdair glanced over his shoulder as if to make certain she wasn't nearby. "'Tis as though she's in my head and knows what I'm thinking. I don't like it."

Jake wore a crooked smile when he explained, "Their way to handle it is to keep their distance. But Dyna always finds them, faster if they're about to get into trouble."

"Anything else changed since I last left? All are hale?"

"Aye, no changes. What of you? You seemed interested in the Matheson lass the last time I saw you. That has ended?" Jake's warhorse trotted next to Padraig's steed, seemingly enjoying the cool summer evening.

"There are...obstacles. I am interested in her, but she was betrothed years ago by her father. Marcas has ended the agreement, but her betrothed won't relent." He was surprised when Jake reined in his horse to face him.

"You don't strike me as someone who runs when things get difficult, Padraig. What's the true reason you left?"

Padraig cleared his throat, surprised that Jake was so intuitive. Perhaps he'd gained that skill from his sire, too. There was no lying when you stood in front of Alexander Grant. He could see into the roots of you, all the way to your toes.

Padraig stared straight ahead, not wishing to see any judgment pass through his cousin's eyes. The Grants fought with honor but also fought for what was right. Fighting for Gisela should have been the right thing to do.

But she'd walked away from him when he had proposed. Had it been fear driving her actions? Or his?

"Her betrothed has a well-earned reputation. He's known as the Scourge of Black Isle. He beat a lass from another village just to send a message to me and Gisela."

"The message?" Jake asked, his brow raised with curiosity, Alasdair not far behind and listening to every word.

"The Grant warrior needed to go back to Grant land, or more innocents would be harmed. His sire would take no action against him or to control his actions."

"So you left." Jake stared at the reins in his hand then turned his gaze to the forest around them. Padraig could tell he was thinking over his words. Only Jamie reacted quickly to information he received. Jake and Connor both acted exactly like their father, giving every word careful consideration before speaking. "Understood."

They continued on, the wondrous Grant Castle coming into view, the one sight that often caused a lump to form in the back of Padraig's throat. Majestically seated at the top of a hill, it overlooked the village, a loch in the distance, and meadows all around. A huge archery field, an area slated for festivals, and fields for planting grains and vegetables dotted the rocky ground of the Highlands. It was well chosen by their Grant ancestors as one of the few areas that could support many families.

The castle had originally only had two towers, but the brothers had added towers over the years and expanded the keep in order to hold more of their immediate family. Outbuildings and the stables surrounded the courtyard and spilled out past the curtain wall.

But his favorite part? The landscaping. It had started with Aunt Brenna and Aunt Jennie, but Aunt Maddie had continued with the plantings, attempting to add beauty in all the seasons. Fruit trees were plentiful through the village, something else the clan had done right.

He loved Grant Castle and his clan, just not the warrior life. As they approached, he could see some villagers tending Aunt Maddie's colorful flowers at the corners of the towers, something they did out of respect for their mistress. More were inside the castle, especially near the doorway.

"Leaving was a difficult decision," Padraig said. "Do you truly understand? Will most of our clan think I ran away?"

Jake said, "I am the practical one, unlike Connor or Jamie, who both allow emotion to control them. You had no guards with you, and Clan Matheson still struggles from their losses from the curse. Did you have the numbers to go up against the Scourge's clan?"

"Nay."

"What clan is he from?"

"Clan MacKinnie. He's the youngest son. But his sire is concerned because he is acting out of character, says his son has changed of late— leaving for significant lengths of time, more argumentative. We suspect he attacked a lass from Clan Milton and left her in the forest to die, though she refuses to identify her assailant. He has become unpredictable. I don't know what will happen once he learns I've gone. But he threatened to do more if I did not leave. 'Twas the message the beaten lass gave us."

Alasdair said, "Papa, do you not think we should bring an army of Grant warriors to fix the man? 'Tis dishonorable to treat women that way. Grandmama would be verra upset to learn of this."

"Aye, you are correct, Alasdair." Then he turned his attention back to Padraig. "Mayhap we'll consider such an action, but should discuss all of this with your father and mine, along with Jamie and Connor. And it would be rude to go without Clan Matheson's agreement."

"Aye. The situation is too big for one man," Padraig said.

"Forgive me if I'm too bold, but are you interested in a betrothal yourself?" Jake asked as they arrived at the stables, others shouting greetings to Padraig. He hopped off his horse, taking the time to move inside the stable where all the descendants of Uncle Alex's horse Midnight were kept. He grabbed two bunches of dried apples and brought them out to their mounts, knowing Alasdair took care of his own horse, feeding them the treats before the stable lads led them inside to be brushed down.

"'Tis too soon, I believe." He wasn't about to admit his failure. He hadn't gotten used to it himself. "We both agreed we need time to get to know each other. And while I care for her verra much, I am not interested in a wedding that came to be out of fear. I wish it to be a celebration of the happiness of two people. Not to say I wouldn't marry the lass if it would bring peace and prevent harm."

"Didn't stop Marcas and Brigid, did it? Jamie and Gracie married under forced conditions. I don't think he has any regrets."

"Nay, but Brigid chose well, and Jamie and Gracie grew up together. I have strong feelings for Gisela, but much has happened in her life of late. I thought it best if I stepped away for a bit."

"Time will tell," Jake answered, stroking his horse's neck.

"I'm not sure I understand what you mean, Jake."

"Simple. See how long you miss her. A day? Two days? A fortnight? If she doesn't pass from your mind, you'll know she's right for you."

Her saucy lips had crossed his mind several times already. But he also missed their conversations, something he rarely had with other lasses. He missed holding her in his arms, wished she'd be by his side in the morn. They could talk about anything. He and Gisela had discussed the world, the isle, Scotland, their clans, even having bairns. They never ran out of topics to discuss. Aye, he missed her and couldn't fathom not wishing her close.

His cousin Kyla came up to them just as they stepped out of the stables. "Ah, Padraig! Welcome home. You're just the man I need. I know you just arrived, but could you come help me and your mother in the healing chamber?"

"Me? I'm not a healer." He'd never considered himself a healer, even though he'd worked with his mother often, even before she became the Grant healer after Aunt Jennie's marriage to Aedan Cameron.

"Mayhap not," Kyla replied, crossing her arms. "But there's a wee warrior in there who needs convincing to allow your mother to do as she wishes."

Jake barked out a laugh. "And would that wee warrior be related to you, sister?"

Alasdair replied, "I'll go help Alick."

Jake grabbed ahold of his son's tunic from behind. "Nay, you'll leave this to Aunt Kyla and Padraig. Go find Els and see what happened."

Alasdair grumbled and scowled at his father, but he did as he was told.

Padraig motioned for Kyla to lead on. "Tell me what I'm about to step into, please."

"Alick took a deep wound practicing in the lists, caught his left arm well. He doesn't wish to have your mother put the salve on because he thinks it will make him less of a warrior. I said he must. I don't care to see it dripping green fluid in another day and have him fighting the fever."

Padraig waved to those he passed who called out greetings, but he didn't stop to speak to anyone, beyond explaining he was needed for something important. When he stepped into the healing chamber, his mother's face lit up right away, but he kept his own expression serious.

The chamber looked as it always did, neat and tidy, though with so many pots and bowls about, it was a wonder anyone could remember what was in each one, but he knew his mother to be meticulous. She had fresh herbs already hanging from the rafters to dry for use in her many potions and poultices, the plants bringing a unique aroma to the chamber, the scent of home.

There were three pallets for the wounded and sick, mostly used in the aftermath of battle, but many bairns had seen the inside of the chamber from their many cuts and bruises. The pallets were along the outside wall, with two working tables in the center, one for mixing medicines and covered with bowls and pestles, while the other had two stools for patients to sit on during stitching. This is where he found Alick, his hair bright red like his father's, and freckles all across his nose and cheekbones. Finlay had passed his coloring onto his son, one of only a few-flame-haired Grants. Sulking the way lads his age did so well, he lifted his head and smiled when he saw Padraig enter.

"A warrior to help me. Padraig, please help me."

Padraig hid his smile, carrying on with his ruse of disappointment and concern. He knew exactly how to speak to the lad, having spent many days of his younger years practicing in the very same lists. It was a competitive spot. "Good evening, Mama. Are you treating someone else? I need to see you right away."

Busy at the table mixing something, she jerked

her head up at his words. "Padraig! Are you hurt?"

His mother's concern ramped up immediately, but he gave her a tiny wink and continued. "I took a leg wound, and I wish to have your magic salve to put on it."

He could tell by the glimmer in his mother's eyes that she'd caught on to his tactic.

Alick stared at him. "Nay, not if 'tis a warrior's wound. You must wear it with pride. May I see it?" His eyes grew wide with excitement.

"Nay, you may not see it. 'Tis near a private place. I don't care if 'tis the most noble wound ever received—I still wish it to heal quickly so I will be ready for my next battle. Healing can take forever without it."

"But, Padraig, do you not wish to be able to show the scar and brag of it? Look at mine. She wants to cover it with salve. I wish for the scar and the pride." Alick held his wounded arm up for Padraig's examination. Padraig had no doubt Alick and his two cousins were as fierce as ever any eight-year-old warriors could be.

Jake arrived just then, so the two men studied the wound while Alick awaited their response.

"No worries, lad," Padraig said. "That wound will still scar nicely for you. You earned it fighting?"

"I earned it in the lists. Does that not count?"

Padraig turned to Jake since he was laird and often in charge of the lists. Jake crossed his arms and said, "It counts. Lists or the battlefield. Either is a source of pride, lad. That will scar with or without it, but he's right that Aunt Caralyn's salve will get you back to fighting faster. If you wish to be a Grant warrior, you must ensure your wounds heal."

"Did you use it on your shoulder, Chief?" Alick asked.

"I surely did. She's put it on every wound I've had. My mother wished for it, and I always honor my mother."

Alick looked defeated, hanging his head a bit. "Grandmama would want me to have the salve. 'Tis true. I forgot about her."

Kyla harrumphed. "So you'll do it for Grandmama but not me? Well, whatever works." She tossed her hands in the air and rolled her eyes at Padraig's mother, who just smiled as she fetched the pot of salve from her worktable.

The door opened, and Padraig's great uncle Alex stepped in. "I heard you received a blow today, lad. Good work coming here straight off. Caralyn has treated most of my wounds with that salve."

Alick held his arm out so fast Padraig had to stifle his laughter. "Would you like to see it, Grandpapa? I was stabbed in the lists."

"Stabbed? I think struck is a better word, but it shows you work hard. Now let your Aunt Caralyn fix it for you." Uncle Alex stepped closer and clasped Alick's shoulder. "'Tis the way of warriors, lad. Never argue with a healer. Be grateful you have a grand one."

After Alick was all patched up, Padraig stayed back when the others left, just to greet his mother properly. "Mama, you are well?"

"Aye, Padraig. I am pleased to have you home. I wish you would help out with all the bairns. You are so good with them. A bairn at heart, I think. Come, let's find you something to eat. I'm sure you've been traveling quickly."

He gave her a hug, and they headed into Grant Castle's great hall, greeting those who were gathered there.

Not long after they arrived, his father joined them at the table. "You are home. Welcome. Your timing is perfect."

"Why is that, Da?"

"Because we could use your help in the lists. We have a batch of new guards who need focused training."

"Robbie, please," his mother interjected. "You know 'tis not his favorite thing to do. Can we not allow him one evening of peace? You came from Black Isle, aye? Who came along with you?"

Blast it, but his mother always had a way to sneak in her question. He'd start by ignoring and see if he got away with it. He wasn't ready for the lecturing his penchant for traveling solo always brought him.

"Straight from Black Isle, and I did not slow my journey. I could use some food, if there's anything left of the evening meal. Then I'll retire to my bed if my chamber has not been given away?" He hoped his supposed fatigue would postpone the inquisition and the resulting lecture.

"Nay, your chamber is here, or you can come to our cottage." His parents had always preferred their cottage on the loch to the castle. Though it had started small, they'd added on as their family had grown.

"I'll stay here this night. Mayhap another day I'll visit the loch." He didn't wish to tell his parents the truth—that there could be a rogue warrior named Donald MacKinnie after him, and he was neither polite nor rational. If the bastard had followed him, better to sleep behind the gates so he wasn't awakened with a dagger in his belly. And better not to risk leading him to his parents' home.

Robbie asked, "You haven't changed your mind about the lists?"

"Nay," he said.

"Logan Ramsay said you were a fierce fighter on Black Isle."

"Mayhap I was. I've had the best training, and I've not forgotten it, but spending my day fighting isn't my first choice. I'll not hesitate if there's a purpose, like protecting Matheson land or stopping someone from declaring Jennet a witch, but I don't wish to dedicate all my waking hours to it."

"There are other things you could do. You could have studied with the armorer or become a blacksmith. Both are fine trades. But you were not interested in that. After you fostered with Aedan Cameron, we hoped you'd come back to stay, use your skills for your clan like all the others. Uncle Alex often asks where you are off to and what you are doing. We never know what to answer."

Padraig scratched his head. "I wish I knew

where my road might lead me, but I haven't decided yet. I know you've been more than generous with your coin, allowing me to travel after I returned from Cameron land. I just wished to explore a wee bit." He had planned on settling down, but he was often called to assist his clan in different ways. He'd gone to help his brother Roddy when he'd first married. Had helped his cousin Braden at Muir Castle for a while after he married and his aunt and uncle had moved in, not only with the fighting but all the repairs and rebuilding afterward. Then he'd been part of the force sent to help on Black Isle when his cousins were kidnapped. How could he not go?

"Your mother and I gave our blessings for you to wander the country, see what you wished to do, help your clanmates in their new endeavors, but the English have been bearing down hard on the Scots, ever since King Alexander's death. It was safe to travel alone for many years, but no longer. Your mother cannot sleep at night worrying about you. You cannot keep wandering, or you may find shackles around your wrists and then a noose around your neck. Trust me, you'll not like being put in a dungeon. Ask Loki. He'll tell you how it feels."

"I don't think that will happen, Papa. The English won't bother me. I'm innocent of any wrongdoing."

Unless Donald MacKinnie starts telling lies about you.

Hell, where had that thought come from? He didn't wish to consider that possibility. Would

MacKinnie follow him this far just to get revenge for Padraig paying attention to the woman Donald considered his? Or to make sure he didn't come back for Gisela?

"That doesn't mean an English nobleman won't accuse you of something." His father spun the goblet in his hand on the table, something he often did when he was upset. "I don't want word to come to your mother that you've been imprisoned or hanged. If you wish to stay on Black Isle, then stay there. Or go to your brother's castle and stay. Find your place. But please stop wandering alone."

"You worked with me enough through the years that I'd hoped you might be interested in becoming a healer," his mother said. "You have skills there. Why do you not wish to do that?"

He had enjoyed healing when he worked with his mother, but taking care of warriors, seeing their grievous injuries—loss of limbs, gut wounds, permanent crippling—it had all been too much for him.

"Mama, my apologies for disappointing you." He ran his hand down his face, wishing he could come up with something. Anything.

"You have not disappointed me. I just wish for you to be happy, Padraig." The tears in his mother's eyes nearly undid him.

"You need not worry about me. I always manage to make my way. You know that." He knew his words were wasted. He'd never be able to convince his sire that he was fine on his own. That he'd found back paths to travel, knew what to look out for, and was good at defending himself.

His mother's comments hit him harder. "Your father is right. We hear of more and more Lowlanders being imprisoned for no reason. You love to go to Edinburgh, but even there you must be careful. I don't trust King Edward or his men. Stay here for a while. Please."

Since he hadn't decided where else he'd go at the moment, it couldn't hurt to promise his mother he'd stay, but he wouldn't commit to how long that would be. "I'll stay, Mama."

"For how long?"

He wouldn't give her his true answer, that he'd stay until he felt compelled to go back to claim Gisela as his wife. "I'll stay for a while, Mama. I promise."

"I hope to have you here for a fortnight or more."

"As long as I'm wanted. Does that work for you? You'll wish to kick me out soon, I expect."

He could only hope that Donald MacKinnie wouldn't make him regret his words.

CHAPTER NINE

———◆———

GISELA'S HEART LURCHED every time she thought of Padraig. What was she to do? She'd loved the man more than any other, yet she'd betrayed that love in the worst possible way.

She'd denied it.

How she wished she knew his true feelings. Was Padraig offended or angry? She'd not now unless he was around to gauge his affections.

She couldn't stop the feeling that she'd sent him away.

Not without reason. She feared retaliation against her family, against the wee ones she adored. And she wasn't ready to leave her clan, whether it would be to live on Grant land or to travel as she once wished. They needed her here on Black Isle.

Now her life was in turmoil, and she didn't know which way to turn. She'd always dreamed of the most wonderful man asking for her hand in marriage. At one time, it had been Donald, when he'd been charming and handsome. She didn't know what had happened to change him—or perhaps he was evil at his core, and he'd hid it for years.

She'd had something so many other women wished for—the son of a chieftain as her betrothed—but she wanted no part of the life she would have if she married Donald. From the way he grabbed her and tried to control her, even before they were married, she'd known in her heart that he would only be worse to his wife. And the way he'd hurt Dagga, who had no part in the whole sorry affair, only confirmed it.

Once Dagga had mostly healed, she'd lost much of her fear and gone home to her village escorted by a dozen Matheson guards. Padraig had been gone for five days, but Donald MacKinnie was still out there somewhere. He'd sent no more "messages" and not returned to Matheson land since her brothers had forced him away. So perhaps Padraig had chosen aright.

The door to the hall opened so Gisela lowered her needlework—a winter outfit for Kara—to her lap. Someone she didn't recognize entered—a young man, a little breathless from hurry or worry. He half-bowed to her. "We need a healer, my lady. May we call upon one of the three you have?"

"Yes, be certain of it," Gisela said, gesturing for the maid who had guided the man inside to go in search of Tara. Brigid and Jennet had gone to tend a woman laboring through a childbirth beyond the skills of the village midwife.

A moment later, Tara entered from the kitchen and asked, "Where am I needed? What's the problem?"

"All of my sister's bairns have the sweating sickness, and now my brother's do, too. We have lost my sister and her infant already. We canna lose any more." The haggard man's eyes told the story. He feared for all their lives.

Tara said, "Allow me a moment to get my things, and I'll come immediately. Gisela, will you let Brigid and Jennet know where I've gone when they return? I must be careful not to visit with our bairns for a few days after we return."

"Why not?" Gisela asked, worry for Kara and Tiernay spiking in her chest.

"Sweating sickness passes from one to the other. And I'll not endanger our beloved bairns—they are especially at risk, so Mama says."

"I'll come with you." Gisela got up and put her needlework away. "You cannot go alone."

"Understand you may become ill yourself."

"I understand," she said, swallowing hard. "I cannot do nothing about these bairns. 'Twould be cruel to stand by and allow them to die."

"What about Donald?"

That thought had been raging through her mind, but she couldn't allow others to die because she was afraid of something that may never happen. It had been nearly a sennight. "I'll bring guards along." Still, she wasn't foolish.

Tara spoke to the man at the door. "We'll be ready within half the hour. Have some refreshment and a seat by the hearth. I would ask you not to visit with any of our clan members within the castle. You might carry the sickness with you."

Gisela sent a messenger to request their horses

and the guards then hurried to her chamber to freshen up and pack a small bag, then met Tara in the healing chamber and watched her carefully pack her healer's herbs, tinctures, and various potions.

"You need not go with me, Gisela. I can go alone, see if Shaw can travel with me and bring a couple of guards. I've had sweating sickness before, and I know how to care for it. My mother and I spent a great deal of time testing treatments for it."

Gisela couldn't stay and remain idle. She was too undone about Donald and Padraig and everything else that had happened of late, and if she didn't get out to do something useful, she'd burst. Sitting and thinking about Padraig was too painful, and Brigid had taken over most of Kara and Tiernay's care, especially with Nonie strong again. More and more frustrated with being stuck inside the curtain wall, she had to do something.

"I'll go. You'll need an extra pair of hands, and I'll do whatever you tell me to do." A home where the residents were known to be ill would be just as safe as the castle—even Donald wouldn't risk infection.

"The best thing is to keep them drinking. My mama always said when people sweat, they must replace it. There is no cure for sweating sickness, but most survive unless their fever is too high and they can no longer drink. And bairns are much more likely to die from sweating sickness than men or women."

"Then we should hurry, so we can help these

bairns." Gisela had to admit she found all this information about healing quite interesting.

Tara buckled her bag closed. "Come, I'll explain more along the way."

They rejoined the man, and he practically raced from the hall in his hurry to bring a healer to his family. Several guards, including Torcall, Gisela was happy to see, stood ready with horses already saddled for themselves and the women, and they mounted up and rode out.

They followed their guide through the village and along the path toward Milton land. Just before they reached the border between the two clan territories, they came to a small cluster of homes. Gisela noticed as they passed that while most of the villagers smiled, their initial reaction was to retreat to their cottages.

Tara whispered, "Word has passed about the sweating sickness. 'Tis why they don't greet us."

"So what else can you tell me about this sickness?"

"Och, aye. I forgot. Mama always said the last stage before death is when the body is depleted of water. Everything dries out on the patient— their mouth, their skin, even their eyes. We check their urine because 'tis often the first sign of the body failing. It turns dark from yellow."

"But if it's dark, does that not mean 'tis full of more poisons from your body?"

"Mama used to believe it, but she and Aunt Brenna think 'tis false. Urine turns dark just before death many times, when it stops altogether. We cannot allow them to stop urinating. 'Tis a quick path to death. So they do all they can to replace everything lost in the sweat. That means water. We must get them to drink. And the younger they are, the faster they turn dry. Mama said that, too."

"Truly?" She'd not realized healers put so much time into investigating illnesses and seeking out new remedies for them. What brilliant insights they'd had.

The man led them to a cottage at the edge of the settlement, and Gisela knew it was their destination from the moaning and weak cries that came from it. None of the family's neighbors were outside their homes, instead hiding away. The area was deserted, no people tending the fields, no friends conversing in the path, no lasses or lads playing games. It reminded her of the curse, when most of the clan had stayed hidden in their own homes.

"Have others been sick nearby?" Tara asked the man.

He nodded. "There and there," he said, pointing to some of the homes who'd already had the sickness.

"Have you been ill?"

"Aye, but I recovered. My sister did not."

"My sympathies for your loss. Lead on. Will you stay and help?"

He nodded. "This is my brother's home. My sister's is next door, but we've moved all the ill bairns into the one cottage. My brother's wife is also ill. How can I help? I'll do whatever you ask of me."

"Have you a well nearby? Or a burn?"

"The burn is best. My brother and I will go right away."

"And boil the water on your return."

The man looked confused. "Boil? You will be brewing a special potion for them then?"

"Perhaps. But I also prefer all water given to the sick to be boiled first."

He nodded, though a quizzical look remained on his face. Gisela didn't really understand it, either, but Jennet had once explained to her that a potion brewed with boiling water never caused further sickness, when sometimes it seemed water straight from a burn would. Tara's mother had made the observation and begun boiling all water given to the sick.

Gisela spoke to Torcall before going inside. "We'll be here a few days, I believe. Should you stay or return?"

Torcall said, "I'm leaving two to stay just in case Donald comes along. I'll send a new pair each day for relief and to bring food. I don't want the cottagers feeding them. We can't afford the sickness in our men. Send back updates when each pair departs, and I'll return to escort you back."

"Many thanks to you, Torcall. Tell my brothers we're safe."

Tara opened the door and the two women followed their guide inside. The aromas of sweat and sickness permeating the air. Unable to stop herself, she rubbed her fingers across the base of her nose as if doing so would rid her senses of the smell.

Tara handed her a scarf and held a second in her hand. "Mama wears one to keep the smell at bay. It works well. Tie it over your nose and mouth." Gisela would never have thought to do it, but she was surprised at how well it worked.

"'Tis clearly an improvement, Tara. My thanks to you." The man sought out his brother and spoke to him quietly, then followed him out of the cottage.

A woman—Gisela assumed she was the brother's wife and the mother of some of the ill children—was flat on her back in a bed, looking pale and lost. There were six bairns in various stages of illness, three sound asleep, the rest weeping quietly or coughing.

Gisela glanced at Tara and shrugged her shoulders, looking for guidance. Tara circled the chamber, checking each child and making a quick assessment. When she finished, she pointed to a child of one or two summers near the hearth, her eyes glassy as she stared at them.

"She should be cared for first. Just get her to drink something. Water, milk, anything you can find." They moved to the table and found a pitcher of fresh goat's milk. "Pour some into a bowl, soak this linen in it and allow the wee one to suck on it. Refill it until she'll take no more."

Gisela moved over to the dark-haired lass, who managed to hold her arms up when Gisela knelt down next to her. Her heart broke into at least ten pieces at the state of the listless child. She'd seen similar symptoms not long ago during the curse, but this was different. She wasn't heaving or soiling herself, instead making the oddest barking sound, like the wail of a sick puppy, though she wasn't sure what it meant.

Gisela settled herself in a chair near the hearth, arranging the wee lassie on her lap and the bowl of milk on the nearby table. The lass looked up at her with such hope, she didn't know how to react. Doing as Tara instructed, she took the twist of linen, let it soak up some of the milk, and then set it to the lass's lips.

The girl quieted, and in that moment, Gisela realized what the odd sound had been. The babe had been crying, but she had no tears. She closed her mouth to suckle on the cloth, her eyes locked on Gisela's. It was a slow process, but dose by dose, the lass was able to take in the milk and fell into a peaceful sleep.

The oddest sensation fell over Gisela as she worked, feeding this lass, then the next one, then a wee laddie after that. The better part of the day passed, and she barely noticed, so taken with her work that it seemed the most natural occupation for her—of anything she'd ever done.

If she helped to save these children, she would truly have accomplished something. In fact, just the tiniest smile from the bairns made her heart swell with such satisfaction that she understood in a flash what her purpose was in life.

She was to care for these bairns, just as Tara, and Brigid, and Jennet cared for others. Each of the cousins had her own special talent—childbirth or the wounds of battle or illnesses like this one—

and they each knew the herbs and potions that would help the best. Even now, Tara was at the table, concentrating on mixing herbs in a bowl to brew a medicine for their patients.

Gisela didn't care if she learned how to create the medicines. She just wished to administer them and tend the sick, the helpless, the needy. How rewarding it would be to see them heal and improve.

Gisela settled the final bairn, fed and drowsy, in an open cradle, covering her with a warm plaid, and with a glow of satisfaction, turned to Tara for her next task, the next way she could care and tend and comfort.

Late that night, Gisela bid goodnight to Tara as they staggered toward pallets someone had found for them and placed near the warmth of the cottage hearth. All she wanted to do was lie down and sleep, but it had been a good day. She and Tara would stay until the fever passed and every bairn was out of danger.

"You were wonderful, Gisela. I hope you have no regrets, and I pray we'll not be sickened," Tara said.

"No regrets at all. Only grateful. I may have found a purpose for my life."

She fell asleep as soon as she laid her head upon the pillow.

CHAPTER TEN

———◆———

HE'D BEEN HERE nearly a week now, and it felt as if he'd never left—in ways both good and bad, he had to admit. Before he could take another bite, the door opened and Connor stuck his head in. "Messenger here for you, Padraig. Come out when you're finished, and Jake and I will discuss it with you."

Padraig didn't understand why Connor had phrased it like that and was about to ask, but Connor spun around and left the hall before he could speak. Taking a large gulp of ale to wash down his last bite, he spoke to his sire, who sat across the table from him. "I'll see what it is and let you know, Da."

His father, a spoonful of stew halfway to his mouth, grunted. "I'll be directly behind you."

Padraig knew he should wait for him, but the churning in his gut over MacKinnie and Gisela propelled him out the door and toward the gates, where any messenger would be waiting.

Connor and Jake were already there chatting with the messenger, Connor apparently inviting the man to go inside for food and drink. He could tell by the happiness on the man's face and the lightness in his step as he headed for the castle.

While some might punish a messenger for the bad news they carried, among the Grants, they were always offered hospitality. The meal they received here was likely better than most ever had in their own home.

"Who is it from? Gisela?" he asked.

Jake turned around to face him, a smirk on his face. "Do I detect a wee bit of hope in your gaze? Sorry to disappoint you, but it's from an unknown source. It states you are needed at the northern border of Glen Lochy, near the inn."

"What? Who would send such a request?" Padraig scratched his head. The message was indeed odd.

Connor arched his brow and looked from his brother to his cousin. "I believe 'tis false, especially because 'tis unsigned and they wish for you alone, and in a site of questionable origin. That is not a common meeting place of the Grants, Ramsays, or the Camerons. You need to consider this message carefully before you choose to act on it and follow instructions."

His father joined the conversation, taking the missive and reading it himself. "It must be false. Do not go, Padraig. 'Tis surely a trap, though I have no idea why. I'll go talk to the messenger about who sent him." His father left as abruptly as he'd arrived.

"You'll not go until we find out more, agreed?" Connor asked. "We need to learn more about this."

"I'll await your decision." He looked at the two brothers and nodded to each in recognition of their authority. "I'm going to brush my horse down. 'Tis where I'll be when you decide. It will be better if I'm not to be part of the conversation." He knew if he was there, he would have to describe the true situation regarding MacKinnie. He'd hoped to keep that part away from his parents. His mother worried enough already. And his father would pester him with questions he would not want to answer.

Jake nodded and departed for the keep, Connor behind him. Padraig couldn't help himself, calling out to Jake while Connor moved on. "A moment, please, Jake?"

Jake nodded, indicating Connor could continue on. "What is it?"

"I know it sounds foolish, but I can be there in a few hours. I'd like to uncover the reason for the missive. May I leave and hurry back before nightfall?" He was hopeful. Jake *did* believe in his abilities, something his mother surely did not.

"On one condition. You take two guards with you. Alone under questionable conditions is not wise, but you know that." Jake crossed his arms and planted his feet just so, that position that everyone knew meant he'd not be changing his mind.

"All right. But only two," he conceded. He had to admit that with the threat of Donald MacKinnie out there, it would be best if he didn't travel alone.

Jake gave him the name of the two guards, then

stepped away to speak to the men he'd chosen.

Padraig marched into the stable, grabbed some food, and saddled his horse, saying to the stable lad, "Just taking him for a short trip." The lad nodded and walked away.

Several hours later, he and his men were nearing Glen Lochy when he saw three riders headed straight for him. To his surprise, one of them was his friend Ruari, along with two guards. They met in a clearing, greeting each other with a hand-clasp while the guards stood watch at the edge of the woods. "I see your lads keep you working, my friend," Padraig remarked with a grin. "I see some gray strands hiding between the dark red ones. How are Juliana and the bairns?"

His friend chuckled, "Aye, they are always challenging me. Juliana is well."

"And they make you work harder?" He noticed the man's musculature had grown over the years.

"They do, but enough about them," Ruari said. "What are you doing so close to Cameron land?"

"I received a missive to meet someone at Glen Lochy, but it was unsigned. Curiosity got the best of me." Padraig had a bad feeling that moved from the center of his gut and traveled slowly through every vessel of his body, but he did his best to ignore it. "But I wish to know why you are here."

"Your sire sent a missive to me that you were having a difficult time, with little explanation. I thought I'd take a visit and see exactly what your trouble is about. I surely didn't expect to meet you on the main path."

Padraig sighed, running his knuckles against his

jaw. "Papa shouldn't have told you anything."

"You are not having any trouble? I think you are but don't wish to share. I understand not wishing to worry your parents, but something is up or you wouldn't have been foolish enough to chase an unsigned missive." Ruari took a few steps closer. "'Struth."

"I'm not in any trouble," he snorted, hating that his sire had sent that missive to Ruari.

"The hell you aren't in trouble. Someone has used trickery to get you here, and you obliged them. The question is who and why. You need to tell all, and I'm not leaving until you do." Ruari found a log and sat down, indicating he wasn't leaving.

Padraig moved over to his saddle bag and grabbed two oatcakes, handing one to Ruari before joining him on the log. "I have a suspicion. On Black Isle, I met a lovely lass, but she was betrothed."

Ruari accepted the oatcake and bit in quickly, listening to his story. Padraig filled him in on everything that had happened, then waited for his friend's thoughts.

"He sent the messages. You know that, I'm certain. Why, I'm not sure. But you have proven you have not matured enough to use good judgment yet, my friend," Ruari added with a smirk.

"What the hell does that mean?" Padraig barked, truly offended by the man's comment.

"How many guards traveled along with you?" Ruari asked with an arch of his brow, his gaze searching the area. "Just the two or are there more coming behind you?"

Padraig cleared his throat, not interested in responding to his taunting. His father would say the same, he was certain. He tried his best to glare at Ruari, but he wasn't the least bit offended.

"Oh, I have more," Ruari announced with a grin. "Did you tell anyone where you were off to? Or even that you were taking your leave?"

Padraig scowled. "I did. Jake knows and sent the guards."

"Did you consider leaving on your own? Did you try to convince Jake you didn't need any guards?"

Padraig didn't answer, chewing on his oatcake instead.

"I thought so. You proved my point easily. You did just what that bastard hoped you would do. His trap worked. There's no reason for you to be here, so his motive is still in question, but we'll not stay to give him the chance to think on it. Now, we're getting on our horses and escorting you back to the keep, since you're too foolish to think of yourself as a target."

Padraig had no argument. "You're welcome on Grant land. Stay for a few nights. You know you are always welcome."

"Nay, Juliana would miss me dearly. If I come to stay, it will be with my wife. Mount up, Padraig. I'm not going to sit here as an open target any longer."

He did as Ruari suggested, feeling properly chastened. He'd been foolish and careless. His father would be bellowing from the rafters when he arrived home.

He couldn't help but ask himself the same question over and over again.

What the hell was MacKinnie's reason for the trickery?

The following night, loud pounding jerked Padraig out of sleep. "Wake up, cousin!" It sounded like Jamie.

He rubbed the sleep from his eyes and rolled out of bed, splashing water on his face before donning his tunic and plaid. After all the yelling from his sire upon his return from his unnecessary trip to Glen Lochy, he hoped the elders of the clan hadn't decided to send him away.

His father had been that angry with him.

Opening the door, he looked at his cousin, confused about why he was there in the middle of the night.

"'Tis still night, yes? Is something wrong? Mama? Papa?"

"Aye, 'tis night, but you must come. My apologies for waking you, but you are needed immediately." The expression on Jamie's face was quite somber, not an encouraging sign.

Jamie's words didn't make him any less confused, but since Jamie was one of the lairds, Padraig wouldn't refuse him. Stumbling down the stairway, he was surprised to see a small group of men gathered near the hearth. He recognized some but not all of them. He also was surprised to hear noise coming from his mother's healing chamber.

The group turned their eyes to him. "Is there a problem?" he asked, though he dreaded the answer.

"Aye," one man said, the sheriff of Inverness, someone they were all familiar with, though they hadn't met frequently. "Usually, I need not enter into the affairs of Clan Grant, but since the woman we brought here had a scrap of a Grant plaid in her hand, we need to ask a few questions."

Padraig looked at the faces surrounding him— his sire, Jake, Jamie, Connor, and Uncle Alex. There were two others with the sheriff. "I don't understand. What do you think I might know about this lass?"

Jake said, "A lass was found beaten in the forest. She had a piece of Grant plaid in her hand, and the only word she uttered was your name, Padraig."

"I have not seen any woman but those who live here since I left Black Isle a sennight ago."

"It happened in the early eve. A crofter found her while the blood still ran from her cuts. It had to have happened around then."

Padraig said, "I was here at midnight. In my bed sleeping."

The sheriff's eyes narrowed.

Jake said, "We believe you." He turned to the sheriff and his minions. "He was here all night— and never left. We ate the evening meal together, chatted over by the fire for several hours before we both took our beds. It could not be him. I will vouch for him. Certainly you must find the man who hurt the lass, but Padraig did not do it. We'll ask her when she recovers."

"If she recovers," the sheriff said. "I or one of my men will return to speak with her. We will talk with Padraig again, as well."

Padraig's father stepped forward. "Need I bring up some important points you're missing, Sheriff? Anyone could find a piece of Grant plaid and use it. We have over a thousand warriors who wear our plaid and could catch it on a branch anywhere when out hunting. And anyone who had abused a lass that much would have marks on their hands. My son's hands show no cuts, swellings, or any other sign of having done such violence."

The sheriff stepped closer to Padraig. He ran his eye over Padraig carefully, and then looked to his hands, and Padraig held them up so the man could see them better in the flickering torchlight. "You do have a point. I see only old callouses that every warrior bears, and she was definitely beaten, not cut."

"My son is innocent." His father crossed his arms as if daring the sheriff to question him further.

The sheriff brought his gaze up to Padraig's, who decided it was time for him to speak up for himself. "I am a member of Clan Grant. I do not abuse women. Why would you think I would do such a thing?"

"Sheriff, you know our reputation. If one of my warriors treated a woman like that, I'd handle him before you ever got here," Uncle Alex said, crossing his arms.

"And I would hold him for you, Alex." His father moved next to Padraig and clasped his shoulder. "My son would be the first to come to a lass's defense."

Jake held his arm out toward the door. "Take your leave, Sheriff. Your inquisition is over."

The man glared at Jake but then said, "For now, but we will return." He turned to Uncle Alex and said, "My apologies for awakening you all in the middle of the night. Even without the evidence about the culprit, we would have come, since this is where the best healers are found."

Uncle Alex showed no emotion, as usual, and said, "You've said what you must, now leave, Sheriff."

While the sheriffs were capable of scaring nearly anyone with their mere presence, Alexander Grant could not be so easily intimidated, and the sheriff held considerable respect for the old laird. Alex had always commanded the largest army of warriors in all the land and would send however many men the king needed.

No sheriff wished to anger the king.

Jake and Jamie escorted the three men out, but once they were out of the keep, the true inquisition started. His father turned to face him, his expression serious. "See the trouble you could have been in, leaving on your own? If Ruari hadn't made you return, you could still be out there. But why would she use your name, Padraig?"

Padraig had a sick feeling roiling inside his gut.

This had been Donald's plan. "I'd like to see the lass to see if I recognize her." He had the worst fear that it could be Gisela or someone else from Clan Matheson. "'Tis not Gisela Matheson, is it?"

"Nay, I recall her from Brigid's wedding," Uncle Alex said. "'Tis not that lass. This lass is flame haired."

Padraig let out a loud sigh. "Still, I would like to see her."

"Come with me," his father said. "Your mother and Gracie are treating her." His sire knocked on the healing chamber door.

His mother opened it and motioned them inside. "She's spoken a bit more. She was given a message for Padraig. That's why she spoke his name. The man who attacked her said Padraig is his next target. She doesn't know who he was. He wore no plaid, he was verra large, and he said that you're to stay away from Black Isle. And he's coming to find you."

Padraig made his way over to the lass in the bed. One of her eyes was swollen, but the other caught his gaze. She flinched at first, but then calmed. "Who are you?" she asked.

"I am Padraig Grant, and you have my deepest apology if you were beaten because of me. It was not of my doing." His eyes traveled over her, and she looked much like Dagga had when she'd been found. He recognized Donald's handiwork. One swollen eye, a bruise blooming on her cheek, and smaller cuts and scrapes everywhere he could see skin. He didn't wish to see any more.

"'Tis not your fault, but I don't understand why

he doesn't beat you instead of me." She winced at the pain of her cut lip, soothing it with her tongue.

His father uttered one word. "Who?"

Padraig looked at him over his shoulder. "Donald MacKinnie. He did the same to a lass on Black Isle. 'Tis why I left. He said if I didn't leave, he'd beat more women. Clearly he doesn't keep his word."

The lass moaned again and curled into a ball, knees to chest, so they returned to the hall, moving over to the few still near the hearth.

"Did you recognize her?" Connor asked.

Padraig shook his head. "But I know the cause and the culprit."

"Tell us, lad," Uncle Alex ordered.

For the second time that day, he told the story of Gisela's betrothal and Donald's madness. He shook his head as he finished, finally conceding, "'Tis time to take action to stop him."

"We should take three hundred warriors and attack Clan MacKinnie," Connor said. "That will take care of the bastard."

"But he's no longer there. I visited the clan before I left to give him my own warning, but the chief said he had no idea where his son had gone, that he'd left the castle and not returned. He was acting on his own, not in the clan's name."

Alex moved over to the hearth, crossing his arms over his chest. "So we cannot attack Clan MacKinnie because he's not acting on his clan's behalf. If his sire isn't defending him, it would be wrong to take the fight to Chief MacKinnie. We need to send patrols out in search of this fool and find him ourselves."

"Padraig," his father said, following his brother and taking a seat near the hearth, his voice dropping a wee bit as if to make sure they weren't overheard. "You left Grant land with only two guards to go to Glen Lochy knowing all this was taking place? Over an unsigned missive? Did you leave all your senses back on Black Isle? MacKinnie could be out there waiting for you, especially if he knows you often travel alone."

"What exactly did Ruari say when you told him everything?" Jake asked. "Had he heard anything on Cameron land? Heard of any lasses being found in other parts of the Highlands?"

Padraig sighed and ran his hand through his hair. He'd been hoping no one would ask him the same question that had been rolling through his mind. Had Donald been the one who tried to lure him out? Was he that conniving? "Ruari reacted to the missive from Papa. He hadn't heard anything about any lasses, just came because he thought I was in trouble."

"And he was right, nay, son?" His father jumped out of his chair and paced, something he only did when he was so angry he couldn't speak. "Padraig, you better stand back because if you step near me, I'll throttle you for sure."

"Robbie, anger will not help," Uncle Alex said. "Calm yourself so you can think more clearly."

His sire glanced at his brother and took a deep breath. "You're right, Alex. But this bastard could be anywhere, and it doesn't sound like he has any distinguishing characteristics. Large and blond isn't enough," his father said. "I think Padraig should go into hiding. Mayhap travel to visit his brother."

"Run away?" Padraig blurted out. "I don't like to run from problems."

Jamie stepped forward and said, "But if he can't find you, he'll not know who or where to attack next. He knows you as a Grant, I'm sure, so knew you'd come here. He probably is unaware of your brother's castle in the Western Highlands, though he could learn of it easy enough. You'll have to move quickly to be ahead of him, but he'll probably find you eventually. It will confuse him and make him rethink his strategy. And if you're not here to witness the damage he does, it will deny him the pleasure he gets from putting your name on his victim's lips. And he might return to Black Isle if he knows you to be all the way to the Western coastline. How daring and foolish is this man?"

While Padraig considered this advice, Uncle Alex said, "I agree with Jamie. I think you should go to the Western Highlands. To Roddy's place, which is far from Black Isle. He'll not find you there, at least not for a while. And if he does follow you there, he'll be far away from any of his cronies."

"If not Roddy's then Muir Castle," his father said. "One or the other. He probably doesn't know your relationship with Braden. And your uncle Brodie can help. Muir Castle has many more trained warriors than Roddy. If you need guards, send word back to us. But I'd suggest you go at first light."

"That soon?" Padraig asked, rubbing the scruff of his beard with his knuckles. The bastard just would not leave him be.

"Aye, before he hurts another. And we'll send out heavy patrols in the area looking for the bastard. That will send him running or keep him in hiding for a wee bit. If we find him, we'll turn him over to the sheriff," Connor said.

"I'll go, but Mama won't be happy."

"Mama wouldn't be happy if you were the next one brought to her near death, either."

Padraig couldn't argue that point.

He was headed west.

CHAPTER ELEVEN

GISELA AND TARA headed back to Matheson land after four days. They'd managed to keep from losing any of their patients—bairns and mother both. And since they had to isolate themselves until they were certain they'd not carried the illness away with them, they had simply stayed in the village a few more days, helping care for the wee ones as they recovered and the family grieved the loss of an infant and its mother. They'd sent word back to Marcas when the guards rotated, informing him of their plans.

Seeing the smiles on the bairns' faces brought Gisela so much joy. The first lass she'd cared for had toddled after her everywhere, choosing to sit on Gisela's lap every chance she got.

She'd been more than happy to oblige her. The lass needed comfort for her losses and the lingering effects of the fever.

"Tara, I think I'd like to travel with you whenever you have bairns to heal. I enjoyed being there with you and helping to care for them. It's a memory that will stay with me for a long time, so different from when my clan suffered with the curse."

"You may come along whenever you like. I love caring for bairns, but Jennet does not, and if Brigid had her way, she'd prefer to only care for women carrying and delivering babes. We're all different in what we like. I can teach you how to mix medicines."

"Nay, I'll pass. I just prefer to offer comfort and care. You give me instructions, and I'll see them through."

When they neared Matheson land, Gisela's heart sank. She turned around, making sure all five guards were close. Not enough to put her at ease when Donald MacKinnie was concerned, but better than no guards at all. She suddenly longed more than ever for Padraig's comforting presence at her side. "Torcall, do you see what I see ahead?"

"I see, and you need not worry. He'll not touch you. All five of us will surround you until we get you inside. If he tries to block us, Tara will go on ahead to bring Marcas and more guards. I don't believe he'll have any care for Tara."

Tara nodded quickly. "I'll do it. He's not after me." She moved her horse away from Gisela's as if preparing to leave the group.

Outside the Matheson gates, Donald waited, his horse tossing its head against the man's grip on the reins. An older man in priest's garb sat on a horse behind him, and she recognized Father MacKintyre, but she did not see any guards. Perhaps her own men would be enough to get them through safely.

"Where have you been, wife-to-be?" Donald bellowed as soon as they were near Eddirdale Castle.

"We were on a healing mission, helping a family," Gisela said while Tara moved farther away from the group. "But I know you would not understand our desire to help, rather than hurt." Gisela watched Donald's face carefully, but he didn't register the insult at all. No surprise. "What do you want, Donald? I'm tired, and I need some sleep. I've spent the last several days caring for sick bairns. I hope I haven't caught their illness."

Donald ignored her comment, though she wasn't surprised. "You can sleep all you like after we've said our vows and I've taken your virtue." He motioned the priest forward. "Father MacKintyre is here to marry us."

"Donald, I will not marry you."

The priest's face showed his surprise, causing him to stumble for words before he said, "I cannot marry you to someone who refuses you."

"Shut your mouth, old man. You'll marry us if you wish to live." His voice came out in such a snarl that the priest backed his horse away from Donald. "Gisela, you'll agree to this now."

Torcall urged his horse forward, in front of the two lasses. "Allow us to enter our gates. You've already been informed by Chief Matheson, her brother, that she'll not marry anyone just yet, and never you."

The priest looked stunned. "This is a Matheson lass? Donald, you cannot expect her to marry against the chieftain's wishes."

"Silence!" Donald bellowed. "She will marry me now." He moved toward her, but Torcall and the other guards drew their swords and blocked him from reaching her, Tara spurring her horse through the gates.

Marcas and Shaw raced out, and Marcas's fury shone as bright as the sword in his hand. "You've been told before, MacKinnie. The betrothal is off. My sister will not marry you. Father MacKintyre, you'll not be marrying her to anyone. Not anytime soon."

"I couldn't agree more," the priest said, turning his horse toward the road. "I'll take my leave. Should you need me for anything else, I'll be at Clan MacHeth for a sennight." The poor priest couldn't leave fast enough, urging his horse to a gallop before MacKinnie could move to stop him. She didn't blame him. He was a kind man, not the sort who would obey Donald's belligerent orders or force her to accede to his demands.

Gisela breathed a little more easily. No priest, no wedding.

Donald moved his horse closer to Gisela's, though he could not get past the ring of guards. "I'll say this loud enough that your brothers can hear me. I shall return for you soon, and if you don't come willingly, I'll find another way. You are mine. Our fathers made the agreement, and you'll not dishonor my sire by breaking your word. I allowed the priest to leave only so that you can clean yourself up. You're a mess. Find a gown that suits your station as my wife." Then he rode away, not looking back.

Gisela felt the fury emanating from her entire being, as if a fire coursed through her veins. Glancing down at her gown, she wanted to shout that she had earned the right to look messy, that she'd done something worthy, helping wee ones to heal, feeding them rather than watching them die.

She didn't expect he would understand.

Once he was gone, Marcas said, "Get inside, Gisela, before the fool changes his mind. You'll have to go into hiding until this is over. I thought we'd discussed this. I admire your impulse to help Tara, but I was filled with fear when I returned home and found you gone. 'Tis a good thing you had a sound enough mind to take Torcall along. You will stay home until 'tis safe again."

She had to agree with him, but how long might it be before Donald let up? Peering at Shaw, who had an uncanny way of knowing her thoughts, she waited to see what he would add.

"A long time, I fear. Donald won't forget for a verra long time," Shaw whispered.

———————◆———————

Padraig left just after dawn, although he insisted on seeing the beaten lass one more time, hearing the words from her own lips. He also wanted her to acknowledge before witnesses that Padraig had not been her attacker.

The sheriff had returned and come into the healing chamber with him, close enough to ask the question and to hear her words of denial.

Padraig had not been the guilty party. The sheriff accepted her statement, dropped all suspicion of Padraig as the culprit, and heard Padraig's and the woman's descriptions of Donald so he might be on the lookout for him.

As Padraig headed out to the stable, he noticed one of the guards stopped at the gate, talking with Jamie.

The man had a hole in his plaid, one that was square as if it had been deliberately cut.

Padraig immediately changed course to join them. "Pardon me, Chief, but I must ask a question of Eion."

Jamie gave him an odd look but said, "Go ahead. I'll wait." He stood back, crossing his arms across his chest.

"You have a piece of your plaid missing. Can ye tell me how that came to be?" He pointed to the spot and waited for his answer. Mayhap he had no idea the hole was even there.

Eion, looking oddly guilty, pursed his lips before admitting, "Aye, I sold it to a reiver."

Jamie's arms dropped to his side, and he took a step forward, just as Uncle Alex joined them. Padraig could tell the moment the older man saw the torn wool. "What the hell were you thinking, Eion?"

"He offered me a silver coin, Chief. How could I turn that down? I wish to buy my sweet wife a ring at the next festival."

"Get the hell out of my sight," Jamie said. "Go home, and don't leave Grant land or you'll not be returning. We'll have to discuss your place here."

"What did I do wrong?"

Uncle Alex shook his head. "You don't deface your plaid or your clan. And your selfish action nearly caused my nephew to get locked up in chains. Do as your chieftain ordered you and do it fast or you'll be sparring with me on the morrow."

Eion's eyes widened, and he paled, "Forgive me for my foolishness. I'll not do it again, my lairds." Then he hurried down the path toward his cottage.

"There's your answer, lad," Uncle Alex said. "I'll tell your sire and send word to the sheriff, though he knows now you're innocent. Get on your way before more happens."

With a small sense of satisfaction, he set out for Roddy's castle with five guards. He would stop the night at his cousin Braden's home. Sleeping inside the gates of a castle that belonged to someone in his clan sounded like the safest plan at this point. It would only take half a day to get to Muir Castle, then another day's travel to Roddy's home.

He wasn't afraid of meeting Donald in a fight. He was afraid of the lies the man continued to tell about Padraig's actions. Padraig feared Donald would soon kill someone and blame that on him, as well. A dead witness could not free Padraig. He had to have someone with him at all times, to bear witness to his innocence.

When he arrived at Muir Castle, Braden's stepson Steenie was the first one to greet them. Steenie's father, now dead, had mistreated both his wife, Cairstine and Steenie. Once she was free of him, Cairstine had married Braden, and their lives had improved a hundredfold.

The lad had also gained a handsome chestnut pony, seemingly one with magical powers, who had become his protector. Corc, the stable master, had admitted he feared the pony, saying an old soul had taken over the beast's body specifically to protect the lad. While he'd learned to trust the pony when it came to Steenie, he still stayed out of its way. Steenie had named the temperamental wee horse Paddy, and he'd been by his side ever since. Padraig was surprised the pony didn't find a way to get into the castle proper at night, even.

Now, Steenie and Paddy crossed the courtyard together, the boy shouting a greeting, the pony echoing it with a neigh.

"Greetings, Steenie. Are my cousin and my uncle inside or on patrol?" He dismounted and motioned for his guards to take their horses to the stable.

"They're inside finishing their meal. What brings you to Muir Castle, Padraig? And you even brought a few guards with you. Something you don't do often," Steenie said. He noticed Steenie now carried a small sword at his waist, indicating he was in training to be a warrior.

"Aye. Times are unsettled. It seemed wise for this journey," Padraig said, not wanting to involve the boy in his troubles. Paddy shoved his nose under Padraig's arm as if demanding his own greeting, and Padraig complied, running his hand down his namesake's smooth neck.

"Why did you choose Paddy for your pet's name, lad? It is a fine name, of that I am sure, but I never had the opportunity to ask you."

"It came to me. I don't question things that pop into my mind quickly. I know many don't believe that Paddy can communicate with me, but he does. He somehow puts those ideas in my mind when I need them most." The lad blushed, probably because he knew how he sounded, talking about a pony like it was a person.

"How many winters are you now?"

"Three and ten. I know a magical pony sounds daft from anyone but a bairn, but he's my best friend." Steenie's blond hair had grown out a bit since Padraig last saw him and now curled at his collar. He'd turned into a nice-looking lad. His golden hair probably already drew the eyes of all the lasses in the castle, though he doubted the lad returned their interest just yet.

"'Tis all right, lad. I believe in magic and faeries and other things, too. All the Camerons do, also, but I think you know that."

"I do. I most enjoy it when Brin comes to visit with his sire. He tells me about Tara and Riley, all their possible magic powers. I don't know if I believe in all of it—seers, talking with the dead, faeries in the forest—but I believe in Paddy. Mama thinks he was sent by my grandfather to protect me when I needed it most. So, will ye tell me why you're here?"

"I need to see Braden. My guards will be pleased to brush their own horses down, if you help them find what they need. I'll send food out for them later."

"Aye, Padraig." Steenie took off toward the stables, Paddy close beside him.

An old man stepped out of the building just as Steenie disappeared through the door. "Greetings to you, my lord."

Padraig frowned, not being used to being addressed as nobility. "Greetings, Corc. How do you fare?"

"Fine, though these bones are getting old and paining me often. If you're looking for Braden, he's inside. He just went in with his sire for the noon meal."

"I have good timing, it seems. Who do I speak to about getting food for my men?"

Corc said, "I just brought fresh bread out and some meat pies. If I don't have enough, I'll send Steenie for more."

Padraig nodded. "Many thanks to you. I'll join my cousin, then. Steenie," he called through the door, "are you coming inside?"

"Nay, I must check on a few coos in the upper pasture. One was close to giving birth, so I may have to bring her down here."

"Good lad. The more meat you have, the better you'll eat."

Padraig went inside and caught up with Braden not far from the hearth.

"Cousin! Do my eyes deceive me? I had no idea you'd be visiting, Padraig. What a pleasant surprise. I've not seen you in a while. What brings you here?"

"I'm on my way to visit Roddy, so I thought to

break my journey here."

"'Tis good you stopped. It saves you a pointless journey. Roddy will be arriving on the morrow, or so he sent word." They walked together to the head table on the great hall's dais, and Padraig took a seat next to Braden's father, Brodie.

His uncle was as surprised to see him as Braden had been. "Padraig, a pleasure to welcome you. Did you plan to meet your brother here?"

"Nay, 'tis only a happy coincidence. How have you and yours fared since I saw you last?"

They shared all the family news as they ate, and eventually the conversation came back around to the reason for Padraig's journey west to see his brother.

"I hope for his hospitality and advice about a tricky situation I've found myself in." He gave a brief explanation of his run-in with MacKinnie on Black Isle, but he left out his feelings for Gisela.

"There must be a reason he's chosen to harass you," Uncle Brodie said. "I know men like that. Once they have a reason—whether it's a good one or not, or even all in their heads—they won't stop."

Padraig thought hard about how he could most efficiently explain all that had happened, but just as he opened his mouth to speak, the door flew open with a bang. Corc rushed in, clearly upset.

"Steenie. He needs help. One of our herdsmen came back to tell me that he's stuck in the mouth of a cave he was trying to enter."

"Are you sure he's stuck and not just playing a game?" Braden asked. "He does love to jest, at times."

"If you saw how upset Paddy is, you'd know. The beast came back with the herdsman, and he's been snorting and kicking since he arrived."

They left the hall just as Cairstine hurried into the room. "Where is Steenie? One of the servants came and said he's been hurt."

Corc bobbed his head to his mistress. "I'm not sure if he's hurt, but they said he's wedged in a cave mouth. He was trying to get in because he thought he heard a puppy inside. The lad's too soft-hearted."

Padraig took in that information, then said, "You all go ahead. I'll be right behind you." He'd not grown up with a passel of adventurous cousins for nothing—Steenie wasn't the first lad to get himself into a literal tight spot. He rose and turned for the kitchen.

"Where are you going?" Uncle Brodie asked.

"I'll catch up. I have an idea," he explained. In the kitchen, it took a moment to have a word with the cook, who pointed out the bucket he needed. Even so, by the time he reached the courtyard, the others were already gone. One of his guards knew which way they'd ridden, and they set out together.

The place where Steenie had gotten stuck was easy to find, due to the trail left by the many horses of the rescuers. But he also heard the hollering coming from the lad.

The area in front of the cave mouth, which was no more than a slim gap between two rocks, was crowded with a dozen people. Padraig dismounted and waited, listening to Steenie's growing panic, others' shouts for him to calm down, and Cairstine's fretting over her son. Padraig couldn't get through the crowd, but he assessed the situation as well as he could from a distance.

It looked as though the boy had tried to squeeze in sideways but got caught across his middle. His head was able to move and his feet, but his torso was jammed between the rocks, his left arm free on the outside—and probably his right arm free on the inside. If he'd been more plump, they could have squeezed and squished, but he was quite thin, so he couldn't just suck in his gut. That gave them little to work with.

Several men pulled on the poor lad's arm, squeezed him one way or the other, gave their opinions on the situation before they stepped back, unable to free him. Heads shook in frustration. And the lad was growing more and more agitated.

Paddy the pony blew out a snort, as if in comment about the stupidity of Steenie's humans. Then he came up behind Padraig and, using his nose, pushed him forward until he fell into Uncle Brodie.

The older man turned a glare on him. "What are you about, Padraig?"

"My apologies, Uncle. There's a wee beast behind me giving me a shove in your direction."

Paddy moved forward and pushed Uncle Brodie and Braden aside, then nudged Padraig again.

Who was he to ignore a wee, odd horse? He

stepped up for his turn at attempting to free the boy from his predicament.

CHAPTER TWELVE

———◆———

GISELA AWAKENED WITH a pounding headache. She attempted to sit up but found she could barely move. Her head felt as though it would split in two if she tried lifting it a second time.

A female voice called out to her, one that was vaguely familiar, but it made her question where she was. Forcing herself to turn her head to identify who was speaking, she glanced around the room, surprised to see Thebe standing near the door.

She was in a chamber that was not her own, one she'd never seen before. The cottage was small, everything in one room. The bed she was tied to was dirty and old, the musty smell invading her nostrils. It was covered with a thin and lumpy mattress. Her legs and wrists were tied to four wooden posts at the corners, something rarely seen in a cottage. Furniture of a nobleman in a cottage. The hair on her arms stood up when she reached the conclusion she dreaded most.

She'd been stolen away by Donald, who intended to make her his bride.

Thebe fussed on the opposite side of the cottage, moving things around on a table seemingly at random. A chest of drawers stood against the wall, covered in pots, jugs, and other kitchenware. The hearth was opposite the door, though Gisela couldn't quite crane her head around enough to see it well from her position.

She could see the door, a good thing because she'd know exactly when Donald arrived.

Fighting the pain in her head, she mumbled, "Where am I? Why are you here, Thebe?"

"Donald promised me if I took care of you until he returned, that he'd marry me once he got rid of you. Then I'll have maids waiting on me instead of me waiting on selfish noblewomen."

"What are you talking about? Where are we?"

"A cottage in the middle of the forest. I don't know how to describe exactly where it is. I'm terrible with directions. But I only must keep you here until he returns. He loves me."

Gisela's heart pounded faster than her head just at the mention of Donald. "How did I get here? I don't recall."

Thebe giggled. "Of course you don't recall. I slipped a sleeping potion into your broth before I brought it to your bedchamber. Then when you passed out, I let Donald in through the back gates. He slipped abovestairs in the middle of the night. He's verra patient. I wished to move you early, but he refused. Said he wouldn't risk getting caught. And here you are!"

The look on Thebe's face was so happy that Gisela felt oddly sorry for her. She shook off the feeling—Thebe was clearly no ally, though she could easily manipulate the girl into letting her guard down so she could escape. One thing she knew about Thebe was that she was weak in the mind, easily convinced of anything. She'd just have to work some magic on her to persuade her to untie her. Once she was free, overpowering Thebe would be easy—she was slight of build and had always struggled even to carry a bucket across a room.

Gisela had to think through a plan, but the pounding force in her head did not make that easy.

Thebe giggled again. "Donald said I would need to tie you down. He did it for me. He said you might hurt me otherwise." Thebe moved close, just out of Gisela's reach, and looked her in the eye. "You wouldn't hurt me, would you, Gisela? We were friends once."

Gisela tried to reach her, outraged that Thebe would help kidnap her then call her a friend, but the bindings brought her up short. Furious, she spit, catching Thebe's cheek with her spittle.

Thebe swung her hand in a backward arc, slapping Gisela hard across the cheek. "Do not do that again, you shrew." Tears flooded Thebe's cheeks in a flurry, and she spun away from the bed, stomping away to a corner of the room.

Gisela smiled. Then she chastised herself for being cruel. Her father would have told her to make friends with her enemy, and it would be good advice. It was the only way she'd learn Donald's plans and convince Thebe to untie her bonds. Looking around at the small, sparsely furnished cottage, she knew she would need Thebe's assistance to get free and make her way home.

She did not recognize the cottage, so couldn't even begin to guess where they were. She also didn't think Thebe was capable of lying, instead more likely to be proud of the knowledge she could hold over her. The lass had already said she didn't know the location, so she had to guess they were deep in the forest of Gallow Hill Woods or farther. Matheson land? MacKinnie land? Perhaps even Milton land. The cottage was dirty, though Thebe snatched up a broom from next to the hearth and at least pretended to do some cleaning, even as she avoided looking at Gisela. The cottage probably hadn't been used in months, judging by the film of dust Gisela could see on every surface and the tickle in her nose as Thebe's sweeping stirred it up.

"Forgive me, Thebe. I reacted harshly because I was angry and frightened. I shouldn't have done that."

"Nay, you should not have. I was always a friend to you." She stopped sweeping and faced Gisela. "I always loved Donald, you know. Since you don't love him, I should be the one who marries him. I thought you'd be pleased."

Ah, that explained Thebe's story about being in love with a man she could never have. Gisela had foolishly thought it to be one of her brothers and her declared wish to be away from the man an attempt at hiding her true motives.

"Where is Donald now?"

"He's fixing your Grant friend."

A lump formed in her throat, but she forced it back down. He couldn't hurt Padraig because he'd left long ago. Or could he? How far would the man go? "What exactly do you mean by fixing him?"

"I don't know. Donald just said he'd fix him good. Don't worry. He'll be good to him. 'Tis exactly what he said."

How could she explain to a simple-minded person like Thebe that fixing him wasn't going to be a nice thing at all? "When is he returning?"

"Not for two days."

So she had some time. First she had to rest a bit, to calm her headache, to get Thebe's sympathies, then she'd find a way to escape. It wouldn't be hard to trick Thebe into untying her. But she needed all her wits to craft a solid plan.

Sleep, then she'd escape.

———◆———

Padraig didn't know why the damn pony kept pushing him, but once he was close enough to see the fear in Steenie's eyes, he knew it was time for him to act. The poor lad was scrambling to get out and, in the process, was causing his muscles to swell up.

He left his bucket with Corc and said, "Keep an eye on this, will you please?"

Steenie would never get free if he continued to struggle.

Padraig held his hand up, and surprisingly, all

those around him who continued to shout at Steenie fell silent and waited to hear what he had to say. "Steenie," he said, catching the boy's attention, "you can trust that we'll get you out of there, but you're not helping yourself. By fighting it, you're making it more painful and getting more stuck." He could see spots where the lad had already scraped himself raw on the rocks.

"It's hard to breathe. Get me out, Padraig."

In his most calming voice, the same tone his mother used with frantic, hurting bairns, he continued to talk, lowering his voice, slowing it, until his conversation carried a lilt to it, and he hoped it would help calm the lad. He didn't pay much attention to what he said, and though the boy slowed his struggles, he was still distracted by his predicament.

"Look at me, Steenie."

Steenie finally set his gaze on Padraig and nodded, whispering, "Tell me what to do and I'll do it, whatever you say."

Padraig let out his breath in a whoosh, and though the nose of a persistent pony kept pushing at him, he ignored the beast, setting his plan up in his mind. "First, I need you to stop moving. I have a bit of magic that will help to set you free, but I have to climb in as close as I can in order to apply it. You must hold still for a wee bit while I make it work."

Steenie nodded, tears glistening in his eyes.

Paddy nudged Padraig's elbow.

Padraig motioned for Corc to bring him the bucket he'd brought along. While he waited, he told Steenie what he was going to do, still using his soothing tones, hoping to keep the lad calm.

The opening was set right in the hillside, so narrow he never would have tried to enter himself, and he could hear the whines of a pup coming from farther in. No wonder Steenie had tried to get to it. Corc arrived with the bucket and an expression that was half grin, half grimace.

"All right, Steenie. Here we go," Padraig said. He reached into the bucket and grabbed a handful of the pork fat he'd taken from the kitchen. The cook wouldn't be using it to cook with any time soon, but it was a worthwhile trade if it helped get Steenie out of this fix.

"Is that a poultice?" Steenie asked when Padraig massaged the first handful along his body.

"Aye, after a fashion."

"It smells like a pork roast."

"Does it?"

Cairstine said, "Steenie, just close your eyes and let Padraig work."

Paddy whinnied.

Steenie closed his eyes, and Padraig continued to talk to him as he worked. "Do you like pork?" Before he knew it, Steenie was babbling on about his favorite meal. Once he had the boy's torso nearly covered in pig fat, he reached for his arm and moved his shoulder slightly, not surprised to see it slide right out of the close rocks.

"It worked!" Steenie shouted, trying to move everything at once and not getting anywhere. "Help me!"

"Stay calm, Steenie. We have to move one part

at a time. Try this leg. I'll move it a touch." He did, and the hip above the leg was able to maneuver between the rocks.

"Now my arse-end is stuck."

"I'll do it, Padraig." Braden stepped forward, grabbing another chunk of pig fat, and covering the front and back of his body. "There, try that," Braden said a moment later.

With some maneuvering and much wiggling, Steenie managed to free himself from the cave, a weak puppy climbing out behind him with a happy yip.

Steenie reached for him, and the puppy nearly slipped out of his grip, but they all laughed and cheered as the pup set to licking every inch of Steenie he could reach, delighted by the boy's new pork flavor.

Paddy gave a loud whinny, showing his approval of the new pet.

Cairstine hugged Padraig, despite his having his own, less-extensive, coating of grease. "My thanks to you. You were so good with him. Do you work with children often?"

Padraig shook his head. Other than Alick the other day and Marcas's little ones, he'd not spent much time with bairns at all.

Cairstine said, "Well, experience or not, you calmed him down when I wished to scream at him. I do not have your patience, Padraig."

Corc chuckled. "I felt the same. I didn't think he'd ever calm down, but you did it wonderfully."

They moved away from the cave, and Steenie went to mount Paddy, but the horse was not having it. He shook his head with vigor and stepped back.

His mother said, "You're going to have to walk back. You're a wee bit slippery, Steenie. You'll have to bathe back at the castle."

"Padraig, what's in your magic poultice?" Steenie asked.

"Just plain pig fat."

Steenie laughed. "My thanks to you. It's a good thing you were here."

Paddy disappeared, and when he returned, he held something between his teeth. He trotted over to Padraig, who held his hand out, and the pony dropped an apple into it.

The temperamental beast was as appreciative as the rest of the clan.

CHAPTER THIRTEEN

———◆———

PADRAIG KNEW HE'D made the right decision by stopping at Muir Castle. His brother Roddy would arrive sometime that day. He could confer with Roddy, Braden, and Uncle Brodie, tell them the situation, and gain some advice. He just hoped he had come far enough to be out of Donald's reach.

They'd celebrated Steenie's rescue last eve, and he'd had a bit too much wine, but he knew if he ate something, his belly would stop complaining. Heading down to the great hall, he found a crock of porridge and a stack of bowls set out on a sideboard. He served himself, added a wee bit of honey to his oats, and found a seat at a table.

He was surprised to hear footsteps and a familiar voice on the staircase. "You are here, brother. We arrived late last eve after nearly everyone had taken to their bed."

He jumped up, pleased to see his brother earlier than expected, meeting him halfway across the hall. Roddy greeted him heartily with a big hug and a clasp to his shoulder when they finished. "I hear you've been traveling all over the Highlands, even up to Black Isle? Met anyone?"

He peered at his brother, nearly the same size as he was, but Roddy's hair was much lighter, like their sire's. "You've heard already?"

"Word travels quickly, even in the Highlands. Tell me about her," Roddy said as he approached the sideboard to grab his own food.

"I will after you tell me about Rose."

"She's well. In fact, I'll let you in on a secret." His voice dropped to a whisper. "I think she's carrying again, though she'll not admit it."

"A lad or a lassie? Any preference?" Roddy and Rose already had one lad, the eldest, and then a lass, now two winters.

"Whatever we're blessed with. No more changing the subject. Have you found someone or not?"

Padraig filled his brother in on all that had happened, his brother waiting patiently for him to finish with only a few minor interruptions for clarification. He'd always been a good listener, known for giving sage advice, and Padraig trusted him completely.

When he finished, he waited for his brother's response.

"Only you can determine if she is the one. It sounds like you're nearly there, just a few details that don't seem to match up, but if you love her, 'tis no reason not to ask for her hand in marriage."

His pride hadn't allowed him to confess that wee bit, that he had proposed and been rejected. "I'm not sure I understand your meaning."

"'Tis simple. If she loves you and you love her,

you'll find a way to make your lives together. Marriage takes compromise. You won't get everything the way you want it in any relationship. You have to learn to give and take. Are you ready to do that to have her by your side?"

"I cannot answer that yet. Allow me to think on it. I was going to head out and see how Steenie is doing after the episode we had yesterday. Would you care to join me?"

"Aye, Rose is busy with the wee ones and Cairstine and Aunt Celestina are with her, so she has plenty of help."

"I'll tell you about Steenie along the way." Getting up from his chair, Padraig moved over to the sideboard and grabbed an apple and a hunk of cheese. He stuffed the fruit into his pocket and took a bite out of the cheese before heading outside. Robbie followed.

As the two stepped out, he noticed a commotion near the gate, so they made their way over to see what the problem was.

He wished he hadn't.

A voice from the far side of the group yelled out to him. "Are you called Padraig?"

Another voice asked, "Padraig Grant? 'Tis him."

He should have stopped, but he didn't, instead walking directly to the group. "What is the problem? Who is looking for me?"

Braden shook his head and met his eyes, as if trying to give him a silent warning.

A man stepped out of the center of the group, a badge on his shoulder declaring him a sheriff. Padraig didn't recognize him. "Are you Padraig

Grant? The Grant who often travels alone?"

"Aye," he answered, perhaps too quickly. What the hell does traveling alone have to do with anything?

"We're arresting you for thievery. Will you come willingly or must I bind your hands?"

"What?"

The rest of the group quieted as soon as the sheriff spoke. "You've been identified as the man who stole four horses from Clan Haggart down in the valley. One man wearing a Grant plaid."

"Just because I occasionally travel alone doesn't mean I'm guilty."

"We know you travel alone. You've been seen near Inverness, in Perth, and on Black Isle traveling alone. Your Grant plaid has been seen everywhere, even in Glen Lochy. Have you been on a binge of thievery?"

"Hell but nay. When was this act committed?"

"Last eve."

"I haven't left here since I arrived yesterday."

Uncle Brodie stepped forward. "He was with us last eve. I'll swear to it, as will anyone in the castle. Whoever told you he did it is lying."

"My every move is accounted for and witnessed since I left Grant Castle yester morn," Padraig said. "I was nowhere near Haggart land, and I have neither horses nor coin from their sale to prove the theft."

"Doesnae matter," the sheriff said. "I have sworn testimony you were seen. If you can't hold on to your spoils, 'tis not my business. You must come and face judgment." The sheriff nodded to three of the men who stood with him, and they headed toward Padraig. Clearly, the word of his clan, of every resident of Muir Castle, even of Paddy the pony, would not sway this sheriff.

He held his palms up, when one of the sheriff's men raised a set of manacles. "Nay, I'll go along. Uncle Brodie, you'll help me find a way out of this? Roddy, tell our sire. This injustice cannot stand. 'Tis a scheme of Donald MacKinnie's."

Uncle Brodie had a fire in his eyes Padraig hadn't often seen. "Do not worry, lad. We'll find the truth, and the sheriff will pay for his mistakes."

Roddy clapped him on the shoulder. "We'll set things right, brother."

Padraig mounted the horse they pointed to, tied between two larger mounts. It was not a fast-moving horse, that much he could tell. He'd have no way of outrunning them with this beast, even if it were loose.

He was doomed.

The sheriff didn't waste any time hustling the group away from Muir Castle. His uncle's voice called out after them. "Where the hell are you taking him? We have a right to know exactly what shire you're from, Sheriff."

The sheriff ignored him.

Roddy yelled out, "Do not worry, brother. We'll find you and gain your release. I'll go straight to see Papa and Uncle Alex." The sheriff didn't seem to be affected by that declaration.

Nothing more was said until they had traveled for over two hours. Padraig tried again to get more information. "Where are you taking me?"

"The crime was committed in the burgh of Rosemarkie. I am Sheriff of Cromarty, and 'tis my duty to see you punished for your crime."

"Rosemarkie? I was nowhere near there in the past three days. I came from Grant land."

"We'll see."

They arrived at a dilapidated building less than an hour later—and it wasn't anywhere near any burgh or village, let alone Rosemarkie. Within ten minutes, he was locked in a cell with another man. He was given a moth-eaten blanket and a pitcher of water. The cell's sole furnishings were two pallets and a bucket to pish in.

The cell door locked behind him, and his stomach dropped, clenching into a tight ball. "Do I not get to see a judge before I'm imprisoned?"

The sheriff and his men laughed and left without a word. Only an old man remained outside the cell, sitting on a stool not far away. Apparently, he was the only one who would be watching over them.

Padraig peered at the other man in the cell with him. He hadn't bothered to rise from his pallet when Padraig had been shoved into the cell. "Sorry to impose on your privacy. I'm Padraig Grant of Clan Grant."

"John de Bethune. Are you a son of Alexander?" the man asked, arching his brow. Already he'd shown himself wiser than the man who'd arrested him.

"Nephew." Padraig tossed his dirty blanket on the empty pallet and sat down. "What was your crime? And is it as imaginary as mine?"

"I'm accused of killing a man. I was trying to save him by opening his belly to remove a large tumor that would have killed him given much more time, but I failed. He died during the surgery. Now I'm accused of murder."

"So you are a surgeon? Perhaps the first in Scotland, certainly the first I've met. My family has many healers, but no surgeons that I'm aware of."

"Aye, I studied in England, but I wish to practice in Scotland. I didn't reckon it would be such a dangerous occupation here." John sighed, resting his elbows on his knees. He had brown hair tending to curl and looked to be of average height. He didn't have the powerful build Padraig was used to seeing in all the Grant warriors. He had kind eyes, though, and in that way, he resembled the Grant and Ramsay healers.

"How long have you been here?"

"A fortnight. And I've never seen a judge nor had the chance to argue my case or know who my accuser is, though I suspect it is the deceased's brother. He knew my patient wished to attempt the surgery. The tumor was so painful, he didn't wish to go on. He said he'd prefer a quick death from an attempt to rid him of the tumor to a long, painful, drawn-out death. I had all of his family hear him say that—the man's son and daughter, his wife, and his two brothers. But one of his brothers never liked me."

Padraig was stunned. A fortnight without learning anything new? "Do they feed you? You're quite thin, I must say."

"One bowl of porridge a day and a pitcher of water."

Padraig knew he had only one hope that he would get out of here—his family—and he prayed they'd be successful.

He needed his clan to bring a force of Grant warriors to tear down the walls of his prison.

If Uncle Alex and his sire couldn't convince his captors to let him go, the band of warriors could come and demand he be set free or take the walls down.

And he'd forever stop traveling alone.

Frustrated and angry, he wished he had something to punch other than the stone wall. He paced the small area, cursing Donald MacKinnie. He'd known just how to fix everything. This was a false accusation made by a demented man desperate to force Gisela into marriage.

He wondered how she was handling the situation. Had Donald approached her again? Did she know yet that he'd been arrested by the Sheriff of Cromarty?

She would hear eventually, either from their allies or a Grant messenger. He'd guess his sire would be sending a force to Black Isle immediately, hoping to gain information about their sheriff or information about where they lodged prisoners.

He thought of the ruse the bastard had planned to get him away from Grant land, seen traveling alone as proof of his possible guilt in this false charge.

If he ever got out, he'd kill Donald MacKinnie with his bare hands.

———————◆———————

The door flew open, the blast of cool night air awakening Gisela with a start. She again tried to sit up but fell back due to her restraints. For a moment, she'd forgotten where she was. Until she saw Donald MacKinnie looming over her, tallow candle raised high and a broad smile on his face. Thebe had been more resistant to her efforts of persuasion than Gisela had expected, and too much time had gone by. Donald had returned.

"There you are, my sweet one. I'm so pleased to find you here in my bed."

She nearly shrieked, but managed to contain it, though her face betrayed her, of that she was certain. She shimmied as far away from him as she could.

He moved closer and ran a dirty finger down her cheek. He smelled so foul, she thought she might vomit. Then he untied her bindings, for some reason. She was grateful, but she refused to thank him, instead rubbing life back into her limbs and gently probing the raw skin at her wrists and ankles.

What in the world had he been doing? His normal well-combed hair was wildly mussed, and his clothing was streaked with dirt, something she'd never seen before in the vain Donald MacKinnie. This man in front of her she knew nothing about.

"Donald, I don't feel well."

"Don't worry. I'll not bed you until the priest

arrives and marries us. He'll not be here until the day after tomorrow, so I'll just enjoy your lovely company until then. But first I must take a pish."

He strode back to the door, but then paused and moved over to Thebe where she sat at the table. He leered and squeezed her breast before he turned back toward the door.

Thebe sighed. "Oh, Donald. I know you love me best."

Donald threw his head back and laughed as he headed outside, the sound breaking off suddenly. Donald's hands went to the sides of his head for a moment. When he dropped them, he shot Gisela a glare and finally disappeared, closing the door behind him.

Thebe crept close to Gisela and whispered, "If you wish to run, now would be the best time."

Thebe's words echoed Gisela's own thoughts, and she didn't wait. He'd return quickly. She slid her feet into her slippers and opened the door as quietly as possible, peeking around the doorframe to see where he was. The moon wasn't quite full, but bright enough to let her see the shapes of things. Once she caught his back to her, she bolted, flying across the landscape, pounding over rocks and thrashing through bushes without care, sending sleeping animals scurrying and the birds aloft.

"Nay, you'll not leave me yet, my sweet! But I do love a good chase." His voice carried across the forest, lighting a fear inside her, as his voice always did. This time, she used that fear to push her faster and harder. He wouldn't be kind if he caught up with her.

She glanced over her shoulder to see where he was but couldn't quite see him. Nevertheless, she could tell by the sound of cracking tree branches and rustling brush that he wasn't as far behind her as she'd hoped.

She would not stop for anything.

She ran until her lungs were near exploding, and even then forced her legs to move as fast as they could, an arm up in front of her eyes to keep the random twigs and branches from blinding her. His laughter carried to her, but she ignored it.

She broke into a clearing and on instinct, she turned right, her chest heaving now from exertion. Her mind sparking with worry and fear, she prayed she could outrun him and that she had chosen the right direction.

His laughter was louder behind her. He was gaining ground.

Spotting a deer trail between the trees, she followed it. At least she could see where she was going, and perhaps she would find a true road or a hiding spot. Perhaps there was a cave or a hollow log nearby where she could hide until he raced past her.

Something.

Anything.

But nothing appeared. She raced on, her tears breaking through, and she cursed quietly, as the stuffiness that came with them would make it hard to breathe and harder to run.

Donald would hear her quiet whimpering even

if she managed to find a hiding place, but she could not quell the fear bubbling up from deep inside her. Donald had surely gone mad.

His footsteps were close now, the crack of him breaking a branch she'd managed to duck telling her that he'd nearly caught her. He'd be upon her soon.

Kissing her or hitting her?

She didn't wish to find out. She didn't know which would be worse.

A meaty paw caught her hair, yanking her backwards and into his arms.

Donald laughed, a guttural sound that made her skin crawl.

He laughed and laughed and laughed.

CHAPTER FOURTEEN

———◆———

PADRAIG GUESSED THAT three days had passed since he'd been brought to the cell, and other than the old man bringing them porridge and water once a day, nothing had happened.

Nothing from the sheriff, no information about his accuser, no news of when he would be let go or face any kind of trial.

Even his hope of his clan coming to save him was fading.

John explained, "They probably have no idea where to find you. Whoever wanted you out of the way chose this place intentionally. 'Tis well hidden, and no one knows of it but those who brought us here. I lived not far from here for a few months, and I knew nothing of this place."

Padraig scratched his dirty hair. While he'd been able to wash his face and hands, the rest of him was in deep need of a dip in the closest loch. "I don't doubt you. My sire would have had an army of Grant warriors here by now, if they knew." He stood on tiptoes to peek out the one small window at the top of the cell, peering out into the surrounding area.

The sun shone brightly that day, lighting up the area, but all he saw were trees.

A deep forest spread out over the Highlands, part of the beauty of their land—he was sure this was the same forest that surrounded his own home. But the thick trees were proof that one could truly get lost in the beauty of the Highlands, never to go home again.

One could just circle among the trees, the midgies, and the wolves.

He would not give up hope, though. His father would never give up looking for him. His uncle knew what had happened to him, and they would already be searching. Yet finding this place could take his clan days.

Or months.

He stepped away from the window and forced himself to move, to keep his muscles loose and strong. If he didn't, he would soon look like John de Bethune.

"So, Padraig Grant, when you are not imprisoned unjustly, what do you do?" John asked. "The Grant clan, I've heard, is full of mighty warriors, yet you don't seem the type."

Padraig arched a brow, not sure how he should take that remark. "For the most part, I've been wandering. I wished to follow the model of my aunt and uncle, who travel on behalf of the Scottish Crown."

"As spies?"

"Nay, they travel to let the king know who is most in need of assistance," Padraig answered. John was right, but it would be dangerous to admit as much to a near stranger. "'Tis the traveling part that draws me. I've always wished to be like them. Travel the country, see how others live. See the harbors, the farmland, the merchants in Edinburgh. The world is full of so many different people."

"So how do you support yourself?"

"Support myself?"

"How do you earn coin? Or pay your way along the road? Do you trade a skill for food?"

Padraig scowled. Now that he was being pressed on it, he didn't want to admit he stopped on Grant land for coin whenever he ran out. He'd taken full advantage of his parents' generous natures. He'd never realized how odd it was that he did not have an occupation, though he was well past the age for it. He cleared his throat, trying to come up with an answer but wasn't satisfied with anything he came up with. He'd been offered food and drink by many because of his good nature and his willingness to help those he met along the way. And he could always count on the clan's hospitality.

There was the time he helped someone cut down a tree and the time he'd helped another skin a deer, and when he'd volunteered to help a fisherman repair his boat. He'd helped a few build a cottage, thatched a roof or two. Assisted a priest repairing steps to a kirk. That one task had earned him some fine wine.

"I don't have a single trade. 'Tis why I'm in the trouble I'm in. My sire always wished for me to train the Grant men for battle, but spending my days as a warrior never seemed to suit. 'Tis the Grant way, but I wish for a different life for myself."

"How old are you, lad?"

"Four and twenty winters."

John smiled. "So not a lad any longer. Allow me to pose a different question to you. Other than having a romp in the hay with a maid, what was the last thing you did that gave you satisfaction? What have you done that you wished you could spend more time doing, besides wandering?"

Padraig shrugged, nothing specific popping into his mind.

"What about something you did that someone commended you for? Something you did so well that someone noticed, someone complimented your abilities or the way you conducted yourself. There must be something—you seem a capable young man. Build a boat? Hone a fine sword? Hunt a boar down swiftly? Usually, you do something well because you enjoy it."

Padraig had to force himself to go over all that had transpired over the last year. He thought of his time on Black Isle, times with his brother or the whole clan, times when he'd wandered aimlessly. Suddenly, a memory popped into his mind, and he smiled.

"How could I have forgotten? It was only days ago." He told how Steenie had gotten himself stuck and none could free him.

"And you were able to get him out? How?"

"I smothered him with pig fat until he slipped out." Padraig chuckled at the memory of the slick boy, the puppy licking his arm, and the smell of it all.

"Of course it would feel good to save him. It was a good idea."

"Aye, but that's not what I meant." The man's questions had made him realize something he hadn't thought of on his own. "Sure, I'm happy to have been able to save him, but…" Aye, he'd done it for Steenie and for Alick both. "It was the way I spoke to him. I was able to calm him down so we could get the grease on him. Before we could help him, I had to convince him to allow us, just like Alick."

"Alick? Who is Alick, and what happened with him?"

So he told that story as well. "I think it was assuring him that he'd still have a fine scar from the wound that changed his mind. 'Tis a sign of valor for Grant men."

"Ah, the scar is a mark of honor to most men. You have the makings of a healer, Padraig. In both cases, you were helping someone. 'Tis exactly the definition of a healer."

"Aye. My mother is a healer, and I often worked with her, especially with the wee ones. I would talk to them while she did her healing." He sat down on his pallet, trying to pull all the thoughts back from his younger years. "How had I forgotten that?" He scratched the beard filling in on his chin.

"Did she teach you anything else? How to stitch a wound or how to keep infection at bay? How to ease an aching head or an ailing belly?"

"Aye, she had potions and poultices for every ailment. My two aunts are fine healers, too, and my cousins. She's written everything down along with the recipes she gained from my aunts, Brenna Ramsay and Jennie Cameron."

"You can read? 'Tis most unusual."

"Aye, Aunt Maddie insisted. She taught us all, and now some of my aunts teach reading to my young cousins. My sire's family all had to learn because they were healers. My grandmother had a giant book of healing where she'd written down all of her experiences and potions. They offer to teach any of the clan how to read, but most don't bother. We didn't have a choice, though, we had to learn.

"You're a fortunate man, and there you have it. You are from a family of healers. You should be a healer, if it gives you satisfaction to work with the ill. 'Tis a gift for sure." John leaned back on his elbows and stared at Padraig. "Verra few are given that type of gift. 'Tis in your family's blood. You should honor it."

He thought of the times he'd helped with men wounded in battle. "I hated working with those wounded in war. I found that part of healing to be most depressing."

John tipped his head, then nodded. "I knew a man in England who chose to work only with bairns. Called himself a specialty doctor. Why not do the same? Work with your mother to learn more, then take your skills across all of Scotland. After all the bairns I've seen turn ill and die, you could find many to help on your travels. You could combine your skill for healing, your ease with the young, and your wish to travel."

Padraig thought on that for a moment, but a loud banging interrupted his thoughts. The two of them went to their door to peer out and see what was happening. The old man who minded them went to the outer door, looking through its small window, rather than opening up right away.

"What the hell?" he muttered.

"What is it?" John asked, though Padraig doubted he'd receive an answer from the caretaker. But the man surprised him in more ways than one.

"'Tis a pony kicking the door." He swung the door open, revealing the chestnut-colored pony with the white mane, and yelled, "Get the hell away from my door."

The pony spun around and kicked out with his hind legs, sending the man flying. He hit the far wall, striking his head against the stone and crumpling to the floor.

Paddy.

Padraig laughed with surprised delight.

CHAPTER FIFTEEN

———— ♦ ————

GISELA, TIED TO the bed again, watched the cottage door open, and she knew exactly who it would be—Donald. She hadn't seen him for two days, and she didn't wish to speak with him now, but he sent Thebe out to fetch water to prepare him breakfast, then approached her.

Looming in the doorway, he gave her a piercing glare. "You are fortunate that I have more important tasks to attend to before I can spend time with you and finally settle our marriage." He untied her and pointed to the table across the room. "Sit and be quiet. I know you must eat."

She climbed out of the bed, stepping away from him, then crossed her arms and turned her face away. She didn't want to look at him anymore. "I'll never love you, Donald. I did have feelings for you at one time, but no more. I love another. Why do you wish to marry someone who hates you?" There was probably no chance of reasoning with the man, but she had to try.

"I know you love that worthless Grant, but he's not here anymore, so there's no one to keep you from me. And if I'm the only one you ever see, you'll start to love me. I know how to make you love me. You'll see."

Startled by his words, she turned back to him. The look in his eyes frightened her more than all the different ways he'd touched her, handled her, or spoken to her. It was cold and calculating, a look that made her fear for whoever married him and hope that no one ever would.

She certainly wouldn't.

"Just because he is not on Black Isle doesn't mean I won't love him. I can love him if he's on Grant land or on Matheson land. It does not matter to me. He'll be back." She lifted her chin, daring him to doubt her. Padraig would return for her. She was certain.

She prayed he would. How many times in the last few days had she recalled every breath of his proposal and her denial? How would she feel if he'd denied her?

Then she thought of how they'd parted. He said it wasn't their time, that someday he'd return. Hadn't he? Every thought, every memory was becoming muddled in her mind.

"He cannot return for you if he's dead, can he?" Donald smirked, an expression of utter confidence. "Or worse," he whispered.

Red fury rose in her at his threats, though she didn't know what could possibly be worse than death.

She ran at him, her nails catching his cheek, drawing blood. Screaming at him, she scratched until he roared and retaliated with a swing, knocking her to the floor with a blow to the side of her head.

Immediately regretting his act, he bent down and cupped her cheek, even helping her stand. "You must behave yourself, or you make me do such things. I didn't want to hurt you. I love you, Gisela. You are the only one for me. But you must do as I say and not anger me."

She waited until his guard was down, then kicked him between his legs. He fell backwards and grabbed his private area. She launched herself toward the door, running the same direction as before. When he'd brought her back the other day, she'd taken the time to look around her for any landmark or sign of where she was, and she'd thought she'd caught sight of a cave in the distance. If her lungs would hold out until she reached that point, she would have a chance.

Plunging through the shrubbery again, holding her arms up to stop the thrashing of the bushes, she ran and ran, praying she could get away from him. Sick to her stomach at the thought of Donald killing Padraig, she recited prayers in time with the beating of her feet—to get away, to stop Donald, to save Padraig's life.

But it wasn't to be. Her legs were already tired from her last run, weak from her time tied to the bed, and they gave out on her, forcing her to her knees twice before Donald finally caught her with a roar.

He shoved her forward until she fell to the ground. Then he was upon her, wrenching her onto her back, the fury in his gaze entirely new.

He was going to kill her.

He held both her arms over her head. "Behave! If you won't do it to protect your own life, perhaps you will for your niece's. Would you like me to bring Kara's dead body to you, or would you prefer to watch me when I do it?"

She lost all control. Kicking and spitting, twisting and fighting for all she was worth.

The last thing she remembered was his fist flying toward her face.

Her world turned blessedly dark.

———◆———

"Paddy!" Padraig shouted in relief.

"You know this animal?" John asked, a wonderful expression of hope on his face.

"He belongs to the lad I saved from the cave. The one I told you about. This is his prized pet."

Paddy lifted his face and showed them his teeth—perhaps expressing his belief that Steenie was *his* pet, not the other way around—before he moved over to the wall where the keys hung. The pony gripped them with his teeth and brought them over to Padraig.

"By God! He's part human, is he not?" John asked him, wide-eyed. "A blessing for sure. I'll not question him at all."

Padraig reached through the window and grabbed the key ring, fumbling with the keys a bit before managing to fit the correct one into the keyhole and releasing them from the cell. Paddy gave a loud whinny and spun toward the door, and they followed him out, the caretaker still out cold.

John leaned over and felt for a pulse before they left. "He's alive. We must hurry before he awakens."

Paddy never looked back, instead leading them down a path through the wilderness, eventually stopping in a clearing where two horses awaited them, a small sack of food, a sword, and two daggers neatly stacked on the ground. When Padraig moved closer, he was shocked to see that one was his own horse, Midnight Blue.

"Paddy, you're a miracle worker," he shouted, running to pat his beloved horse, smiling at the beast's soft nicker. "I'm glad to see you, too, Blue." He glanced over at the other horse and recognized it as a horse belonging to Braden, a mark on its saddle one he recognized.

John stared at their good fortune, grabbing an apple and biting into it with a moan of pleasure. "Am I imagining this? I've finally lost my senses, have I not? Perhaps we've both died and landed in Heaven together."

"Nay," Padraig said, pushing him toward Braden's horse after he'd claimed the sword and tethered it to Blue's saddle. "Get on. We have to move quickly. We can eat later. Paddy has been known to do some magical things before. Just accept it, and let's go before the caretaker comes after us."

They mounted and headed toward a break in the trees, but Paddy snorted at them, leading them the opposite way. Padraig turned his horse to follow without question.

"You truly are trusting this pony?" John called

as he urged his horse to keep up.

"He's gotten us this far, has he not? Why stop now? The stable master who cares for him believes he carries an old soul inside him. He believes everything Paddy does. Found a lass stuck in a snowbank once. Don't question, just follow."

They followed the pony to a main path, and John laughed when he saw it. "Are you going to ask him where we're going?"

"Do you think he'll answer?" Padraig asked with a smirk. Paddy nickered ahead of them as if to laugh himself at their conversation. "Based on what I'm seeing, it seems he's taking us to Grant land. We'll be safer there than Muir Castle, where they arrested me. The sheriff won't dare question my uncle Alex. They all know the size of his army and that he is friends with John Balliol, our new king. Just pray we get there before the sheriff catches up with us. If I see one good landmark, I'll know the rest of the way."

Not long after, he spotted a boulder along the side of the road that told him exactly where they were, and to his relief, they made it to Grant land without seeing another soul. He could see a trio of three horses approaching them from a distance, almost as if their presence had been sensed. A moment later, his father, Uncle Brodie, and Connor rode up to them.

"You got away?" Connor asked. "We've had patrols out searching for days!"

"Who is with you?" his father asked.

"And what does Paddy have to do with this?" Uncle Brodie asked.

"It wasn't so much that we escaped as Paddy rescued us." Padraig introduced John and told the story of their escape quickly, still uneasy about any pursuit that might be behind them. "He had these two horses waiting for us."

Uncle Brodie and his father just stared at each other for a moment, then his uncle said, "I'll send a message to Braden. They're searching for you, too, and Steenie will be worried about his pet. And they're probably wondering about the missing horses." He shook his head in bemusement.

When they arrived at the castle, Padraig and John dismounted as soon as they were inside the gates, while Paddy headed straight for the stables. Padraig introduced everyone to John and told his story of false imprisonment yet again.

"Many thanks for your hospitality," John said. "I think I'd better thank the pony who saved us." He headed toward the stables, stopped for a moment with his hands on his hips, then turned back to them and said, "I still can't believe this pony accomplished what he did."

Uncle Brodie laughed. "Never question Paddy. Just thank him."

Padraig followed John and heard Paddy's nicker coming from one of the last stalls at the far end of the stable. One of the stable lads yelled for help. "Who does this pony belong to?"

Padraig raced down to the stall and stopped, laughing. Paddy stood next to a smaller pony filly, and he looked to be whispering in her ear. "Leave her alone, Paddy, she's barely more than a yearling."

Paddy sighed and marched toward the apple bin.

"My thanks to you, Paddy," John said as the pony went past him.

Paddy turned and looked at both of them. Padraig moved up to the old pony and rubbed his ear. "I appreciate all you did, Paddy. Steenie will be verra proud of you."

Paddy nuzzled his hand and pushed against him, looking for more caresses. Uncle Brodie and Padraig's father stood in the stable door watching, both wearing bemused smiles. Uncle Brodie moved over and rubbed the pony's muzzle.

"You are amazing, Paddy. You'll always surprise me." Uncle Brodie nodded to Padraig and said, "Go inside. I'll take care of Paddy and take him home when I go. You both look like you could use some good food and a rest. Mayhap an ale or two."

Padraig stepped into the courtyard and scanned the area, taking in the castle, all his family, and the beautiful sky above.

John stood next to him. "'Tis a most impressive castle."

Padraig saw everything with a clear eye now, a fresh sense of gratitude for his clan and freedom. "Aye, it surely is beautiful."

His father glanced at him and arched a brow, perhaps surprised to hear such a comment from his prodigal son.

"I'll explain everything if we could have something to eat first, Da."

"Of course. I thought for a moment my ears

deceived me. It sounds like you are glad to be home," his father said with a smile.

"I am. More than you know. And I promise never to travel alone again."

CHAPTER SIXTEEN

G ISELA LIFTED HER head from the bed. Her vision swam for a moment but when it cleared, she could see Thebe fussing with something on a nearby table. A tentative tug with a hand and foot told her she was tied yet again.

"Thebe, is he still here?"

The maidservant spun around. "Nay, he left."

"Not for Kara. Please tell me he'll not hurt my niece." Her heart nearly ripped out of her chest at the thought of anything happening to the bairn. "Even you must see that this should not affect a child. You loved Kara, did you not?" She had to have Thebe on her side with this, at least.

"I do care for Kara, but he is not going after her. He is making certain you'll never see Padraig again. He's checking to see if his plan worked."

"What plan?" Almost regretting her words, she feared it could be better if she didn't know the depravity Donald could be capable of inflicting on Padraig. Gisela closed her eyes, praying someone would help him, protect him from Donald. "I don't know what has happened to Donald. He's turned cruel, Thebe, gone mad. You should get away while you can. He's changed. Something has happened inside his head. Do you not fear him?"

Thebe gave her the most hateful look she'd ever seen. "Never. I love Donald. I always have, and I'll be his mistress after he marries you. Over time, he'll grow to love me because I'll treat him right. Once he gets you with child, he'll be all mine. You'll see."

Thebe had gone mad, too.

She continued her rant as she fussed at the table. "I think you should continue to refuse him, Gisela. Then he'll come to me."

"I have, and I will always refuse him. Do you not know that?" Was Thebe so in love with the man that she couldn't see what was happening, couldn't hear her clear rejections? "Why do you think I tried to run away?" She had to convince Thebe that she would have a much better chance of marrying Donald if Gisela was out of the way. Though that phrase was not her best choice. "Thebe, if you truly love Donald, then you should go back to Eddirdale Castle, tell my brothers what has happened, and they'll come and get me. Then you'll have Donald all to yourself."

Thebe stared at the vegetables she was chopping to throw in a pot, pausing before she spoke. "Nay, I cannot. He would be so angry with me. I'll not upset him. I won't." Thebe chopped her vegetables a bit more forcefully before she stared up at the thatched roof, tears blurring her eyes. "He's all I've ever wanted, yet you push him away. I love him. I'll never leave him."

Seeing the tears in her eyes, Gisela knew she'd never be able to convince Thebe to help her. She had lost her own senses, as surely as Donald had.

"I love Padraig, just as you love Donald. 'Tis all I have to say. How long before he returns?"

"I know not. Usually he's gone for a day at a time, mayhap two days. I'll welcome him back into my arms, whenever he returns." Her face lit up with excitement. "And if I'm lucky, I'll be carrying his bairn before long. Perhaps then he'll let you go himself."

Gisela was grateful he had a woman to take care of his needs. How she prayed he'd continue to be satisfied with Thebe and stay away from her.

"The priest should be here on the morrow," Thebe said, a distant sound to her voice. "I may not have much time." She stared at Gisela in an odd way.

Gisela didn't have much time either, and she had the sudden feeling that she needed to fear Thebe as much as she did Donald.

Or more.

———————◆———————

"We'll feed you well, but I'm guessing you might like a bath first?" his sire stated, taking a step back from him.

"Aye, I know how we present. As soon as I grab clean clothes, we'll go visit Aunt Maddie's bathing chamber."

"If I had any coin, I'd pay it all for a tub bath. I'll even gladly jump in the nearest loch, if someone could give me clean clothes." John said to the group. "The conditions in our cell were not the best."

"No one is using the bathing chamber abovestairs," his mother said. "Since 'tis summer, there's plenty of warm water in the buckets."

John looked at Padraig. "Buckets?"

"A pully system to bring them up to the top floor. Something Uncle Alex had made for Aunt Maddie the first winter we were here," Padraig explained. "There are several tubs."

"It would be greatly appreciated."

It didn't take long to get the baths ready, much to Padraig's relief. And an hour later, he and John, washed and shaven, ate heartily with the Grant clan surrounding them.

"John, I'd be honored if you would discuss your skills with me later," Padraig's mother said. "We could share things we've learned from our separate experiences. I always wish to learn more about my calling and how to better help people."

John swallowed his bite before answering. "Aye, I'd be happy to, but perhaps on the morrow after I've had a good night's sleep on a comfortable bed.

Once they finished, Padraig's father motioned him into the healing chamber, his mother following, while John made his way abovestairs to his bedchamber.

"How long was John held in that cell?" his sire asked. "He looks like a skeleton."

"He thought around a fortnight before I arrived, and we were only fed one bowl of porridge each per day. I stopped noticing the hunger after a little while, like my belly knew nothing more would be coming."

His mother let out a deep sigh. "What would we have done without Paddy? After Brodie told us what happened, we sent patrols out, searched for the one who arrested you, but with no luck. We had no idea where you were. Alex put a request in with the king, a formal request for an investigation, but I still don't understand how you ended up there. What happened, Padraig?"

His father took his mother's hand and settled her in a chair at the table, encouraging Padraig to sit as well. "Easy, Caralyn. Give our lad the chance to think. After such an experience, 'tis difficult to get one's thoughts together."

"My apologies, Padraig. Whenever you are ready." She folded her hands in her lap, but her gaze stayed on him. He understood. She was afraid he would disappear. He'd felt that way about Gisela once.

Padraig told them almost the whole story, from the moment he first saw Gisela to Paddy's daring rescue that day.

His mother ran her hand through her hair, fiddling with the strands the same color as his own, even with the few gray hairs mixed in. "I'm happy you have found someone, but if you love the lass, why did you not just propose and marry her? That would be the easiest way to end Donald's claim."

Padraig crossed his arms in front of him. He'd left that part out because it was embarrassing, but at this point, there was no place for lies or omissions. "I did. She turned me down. I asked her to leave with me and we could travel the land, but she said she couldn't leave Clan Matheson. She feels she needs to be there for her niece and nephew, to ease the loss of their mother and transition them to Brigid as their stepmother. She was reluctant to leave her brothers. The lass has a strong sense of clan loyalty. And something else."

He stared up at the ceiling thinking of the bastard who'd forced him out.

His mother said, "I think she'll learn to appreciate you while you're gone. Mayhap she'll change her mind in a short bit."

He stared directly into his mother's eyes. "She was afraid he'd go after her niece and nephew if I stayed. She'll not consent to leave Eddirdale until she's certain they're in no danger."

His mother gasped. "He is that depraved?"

"He is. They say he's changed. Every time I see him, his hand is at his head, as if it pains him. Know you of any sickness like that? And would it change a person that much?"

"I do." They all started at the voice that came from behind them. John stood at the open door. "Apologies for the interruption, mistress, but I think I might be able to help. I couldn't sleep and came to find the comfort of good company after so long alone, and it seems I might be able to offer something in return. May I join your discussion?" He approached the group around the table.

"Please, sit down. I would love to hear your insight," his mother said. "And you must call me Caralyn."

"Many thanks, Caralyn. Aye, Padraig, there's a condition I've seen once or twice before and discussed with other physicians that can change a man in terrible ways. Oddly-placed growths can attach to many different organs, some to the lungs, or the intestines—like the one I attempted to remove from the patient whose brother accused me of murder. Sometimes those growths occur in the brain or under the skull. Depending on exactly where it is, it can change a man's personality completely."

"I recall something similar," his mother whispered, sadly. She dropped her gaze, and Padraig watched the memory play out in phases across her face. Could he ever possibly understand all she'd gone through, all she'd seen as a healer? "I had a patient who was a young father and the sweetest man. In a short time, he turned nasty, cruel. His entire behavior changed."

"Why? Did you ever discover the reason?" Padraig asked.

She nodded, a brief flit of embarrassment crossing her features. "Aunt Brenna was here at the time. She thought it could be a growth in his head, as John described. We couldn't do anything about it—none of our medicines had any effect, and we didn't have the skill to open his head while he lived. He died within a few weeks, and Brenna opened his head to check. She found a growth the size of a chestnut. Turned him daft, she said."

"There's another sign we see most often with these kinds of patients," John said. "Head pains.

Their heads would ache so badly that they would often hold their heads and scream. Many surgeons spoke of keeping them sedated until they died."

"Is there a cure for such a growth?"

John shook his head. "There's nothing to be done. A growth like that will kill eventually, but it can be hard to predict how long before they pass."

So if Donald had that type of sickness, he could continue for a while. "Could it worsen?"

His mother nodded. "Aye, Aunt Brenna said they will continue to grow, and symptoms worsen as time passes. Eventually the pain becomes debilitating."

Padraig paced the room, torn by regret and uncertainty. "When I chose to leave Black Isle, it was because I didn't wish any more women beaten because of me. And I knew Gisela wasn't ready for marriage. I didn't wish our wedding to be tainted with fear. I'd prefer to wait until we can marry without fear, and with laughter. I stand by that decision, but being locked in a cell has changed my thinking in many ways. I should have stayed. If he followed me all the way here, and then to Muir, what good did it do to leave? But I also believe Gisela needed time to listen to her own heart."

"She had much to trouble her heart this past year," her mother said. "'Tis always right to let a lass heal after such a time."

"Verra true. I think she needs to be free of Donald's threats. I could see the strain it caused her." Should he return? Not run away but go back to her? He needed time to think on it all. And he needed rest first. His own heart was nowhere near at ease.

"If you indeed love the lass, then live there, Padraig." His father stood and clasped Padraig's arm. "If you're there with your cousins, you won't feel like an outsider. It's less than two days' ride away, so we can visit you easily, and given time, she'll see your paths lie together."

Padraig stared off into space, thinking over this possibility. It was sound advice, if he just knew how he'd earn his keep. Becoming a warrior for the Matheson clan held no more appeal than life as a Grant warrior. He almost laughed at the idea of him trying to farm a plot or learn a craft.

"What is it?" His mother leaned forward to grasp his hand.

"I can guess," his father said. "You still don't know what you wish to do with your life. Do you still wish to travel?"

"We talked about this, remember?" John asked, giving him a nod of encouragement.

"I do still wish to travel, but not so aimlessly. And no longer alone. I've learned my lesson about that." He stared at his hands, thinking of all they'd discussed. "And thanks to John, I've learned to see my talents are what I'm most drawn to."

"Wonderful." His mother's face lit up. "And what is it that pulls you?"

"Still being like your uncle?" His father's eyes widened in inquiry.

Padraig shook his head. "Nay. I've discovered I like working with bairns and young people. Like with Alick last week and Steenie in the cave."

"Aye, you are good with the young. 'Tis why I wanted you in the training grounds with the boys."

"And something else I realized." He turned his attention to his mother and grasped her hands across the table. "I enjoy healing. I learned so much working with you, Mama. But I never liked working with warriors. It was the bairns I found rewarding."

His mother's voice caught. "Oh, Padraig."

"John says there is a physician in London who only works with bairns. He doesn't treat adults. I think I might like to do that."

His mother clasped her hands together, and to his surprise, tears misted her eyes. "You would be wonderful, especially the way you love to laugh and jest. 'Tis a gift in my eyes. And from what I've heard about Gisela, she loves bairns, too. Could she not work with you?"

John said, "Aye, you could travel and heal bairns. Some healers travel all the time. There's much sickness out there. The man who works just with bairns is kept verra busy. You will never lack for patients."

Padraig had never considered such a possibility, but now he was nearly ecstatic. Had he found his purpose in life? So excited about the possibility, he *couldn't wait* to discuss it with Gisela. He had a feeling she'd love the idea, too.

But they still had to solve their looming problem: Donald.

Padraig was sure the man was lying in wait

for him somewhere between Grant land and Eddirdale Castle. He had to get back to Gisela, which meant avoiding any more traps. He'd not travel alone, and he'd not give himself up so easily as before.

No more cells for him.

CHAPTER SEVENTEEN

———————◆———————

PADRAIG AND HIS cousins sat at one of the largest tables in the hall, strategizing over their midday meal. There had been much discussion about the best way to stop Donald MacKinnie from continuing his attacks on innocent people, but they'd only come up with one solution.

They needed to take a large group of Grant warriors and settle this once and for all. And if they couldn't corner Donald, then they'd take up their complaint with the chieftain of Clan MacKinnie, even if Donald wasn't there. But that move took planning. Jake and Jamie had sent Connor and a few others out to ready the horses and gather the supplies necessary to travel to battle. Connor would be in charge of the warriors, so it was his job to ready the men. As soon as their planning session was over, the rest would join him in the task. And Padraig needed to send a messenger as swiftly as possible to Marcas—he needed to know their force was coming.

It turned out the messenger was unnecessary. A few moments after Connor left, one of the gate guards flew in the door. "Padraig, there's someone here to see you. A messenger from Black Isle."

Padraig nearly knocked his chair over when he bolted off it.

Dear Lord, please don't let it be another sheriff.

That thought sent him racing to the door, not surprised—and not a little relieved—to see his father and Jake follow him. He was glad to have their swords at his back, even if it wasn't the laird's job to know all that took place on Grant land.

As he crossed the courtyard, his belly did somersaults, the dread and fear building inside him.

Had Donald found Gisela?

Had the bastard attacked another woman?

Had he invented another false accusation?

As if he were able to read his mind, his father declared, "No one will be removing you from Grant land, Padraig. Even if the king himself comes for you."

He hoped his father was right.

But it was Torcall waiting outside this gate with his weary horse, not a sheriff.

"Allow him in," Padraig said to the Grant man blocking his way. "He's a Matheson guard and a good one."

Torcall came inside, nodding to Padraig. "Marcas sent me. Gisela is missing. He believes Donald has taken her, possibly to force the marriage. 'Tis actually what they're hoping, that he's taken her instead of continuing to beat innocent lasses. Marcas doesn't think he'd truly hurt Gisela."

His mind went to John's and his mother's words the other night, the possibility of a growth in the man's head. If it were true, then Donald could be getting worse—angrier, crueler, less predictable. He could turn on Gisela. He had to get there soon.

"Has he sent any clear message to Marcas or made any demands? He's a man who likes others to know what he's doing. He always seems to be performing for everyone."

"No, no messages yet," Torcall said. "Thebe is also gone. She told Nonie that she was going home to visit her mother, but she never made it there. Her mother came to the castle to visit her and was verra surprised not to find her. Otherwise, we'd not have known Thebe was even missing."

"Come inside and get something to eat. You're welcome to stay the night, if you like, but if you choose to return today, you'll at least have a fresh mount." Jake said. "We'll do anything we can to assist."

Torcall nodded and said, "Much appreciated, Chief."

Back in the hall, Jake sent a large group of guards out of the keep and into the lists, since the midday meal had just finished. A little more training, and then they, too, would prepare for the journey to Black Isle.

Jake gestured at the serving dishes still on the table. "Help yourself to whatever pleases you." He called over a serving lass. "Bring him whatever he wishes to drink."

Once they were settled, Padraig asked, "Do Marcas and his brothers have a plan?"

Torcall took a bite of crusty, dark bread and chewed, shaking his head. He mumbled between bites, "They were sending Shaw and Ethan to talk to the MacKinnie chief, but Marcas was sure Donald would not be there. Donald would never dare steal Gisela and take her to his keep. He must have her hidden. Patrols have been searching for her but haven't found any sign yet. That was two days ago. He's hoping Chief MacKinnie will send out his own men, since they know that land better. He probably knows exactly where to look for his son."

"Or the bastard already knows where Gisela is and doesn't have to look at all." Padraig looked at his father and Jake. "I'll return with Torcall. I need to help find Gisela." But he was not going to attempt to do anything alone. Not this time— his days in that prison cell had taught him that much. He needed his clan with him. He hadn't needed to worry.

"You'll be taking a slew of Grant warriors with you," his sire said.

Padraig looked to Jake, and the laird nodded in agreement. "Aye, the last I checked, Jamie and Connor had decided on five score. Based on this new information, we'll need to move soon, and perhaps send a second wave."

Padraig stood when Jake did, his admiration for his cousin growing stronger than ever. He was Uncle Alex's eldest, a twin to Jamie, and the two had taken charge and run Clan Grant as well as their sire had. The power their clan held was astounding. At times, he'd been jealous that he'd been born to the younger brother, Robbie, instead of Alex, the eldest of the five Grant siblings, but he'd gotten past that long ago. Jake was far more suited to the role of chieftain than he was.

"I appreciate all you do, Jake," Padraig said, "but especially your help now. The Mathesons are a good clan."

"We know this to be true," Jake said, clasping Padraig's shoulder on his way out. "And I'm always here to support my cousins. Remember that, Padraig, wherever you are. Though I certainly appreciate Paddy's assistance in this particular incident." He grinned and left, calling back over his shoulder, "I'll never understand that daft pony."

Padraig sat back down, not surprised to see Torcall arch his brow in question. "A daft pony?"

"If not for the pony, I might still be in prison."

"Prison? You?" Torcall asked.

"Aye, we suspect Donald planted a story about me attempting some thievery in Rosemarkie and sent a sheriff after me."

Torcall gave him a slow nod. "The sheriff of Cromarty is good friends with Fearchar MacKinnie. That man could be convinced to do anything for a few gold coins, including put you in prison for a false crime. Hell, the man is a criminal himself. And you said a pony helped you escape?"

"Hard to believe, but 'tis true. I'll explain later. For now, let's make plans for how we can best help."

"First off, give us the important information,"

his father, Robbie, said. "How many decent warriors in Clan Matheson and Clan MacKinnie? And how many allies will jump in to help the MacKinnies fight?"

Torcall looked to Padraig before he answered. "The Miltons will join them. Together, probably three hundred? But 'tis only a guess. We are at well under a hundred men. I think three score at last count, and not all are skilled with a sword."

"Any archers?"

"A few huntsmen and whatever Ramsays are visiting. We have some in training, but they are also swordsmen."

Padraig looked over at his father. "Should we take more?"

"Jake can have a hundred ready to go with you now. He can send another hundred or two later, but it takes some time to get that many men ready to travel. We cannot allow you to go unguarded. Promise me you'll stay with the group, Padraig. If your mother learns of you being held captive again, I don't know if she will survive it. She took it verra hard every time a patrol returned with no sign of you anywhere."

"I've learned my lesson. I'll not risk it again. The men who came for me at Braden's didn't care what my name was, wasn't concerned about Alex Grant. I've never seen that before."

"Too bad," his father said. "They're about to learn different. The whole lot of them will remember our name after we've finished with them."

"I'm happy to see how strong the support of our

clan can be, though perhaps I brought us more trouble than necessary. I was foolish, Papa. Please forgive me for my ways. My days of traveling alone are done. I see the wisdom of it now."

His father slapped his back heartily. "Though it worried your mother, the rest of us don't mind a little trouble now and then. Keeps us at our best."

Padraig gave his father a puzzled look.

The smug look on his sire's face explained his thoughts a bit. They were about to hear a tale or two about the many Grant battles in the past.

"Reminds me of days of old when we were just building Clan Grant. Fools would think we were some wee clan to brush away like a midge. They found out differently when we came with our force of Highland warriors into the Lowlands. Good times."

Torcall looked at the older warrior with awe. "Wish I would be here to hear more tales."

"Another time, lad. I'll coordinate with Jake and the warriors. When you two are ready, we'll be ready." His smile widened, if that was possible. "They may have seen the Ramsay archers, but they haven't met the Grant warriors yet."

Torcall laughed.

———◆———

Donald flew in the door and slammed it behind him.

Thebe spun around and hurried to his side. "I'm so glad you're back."

She reached for him, but he put his arm up, shoving her hard.

"I don't have time. I have to get the priest to marry us quickly. Untie her."

"Us? You and me?" Thebe's hopeful expression filled Gisela with something near pity. Until she smirked at Gisela as she worked at the knots of her bindings.

"Nay, not you, ye fool," Donald growled. Once Gisela was loose, he grabbed her by the arm, dragging her to her feet. "We're meeting the priest on MacKinnie land and marrying this eve."

"But Donald, why the rush?" Thebe asked, tears glistening at the corners of her eyes.

"Grant warriors are coming this way. One of the Matheson guards went for assistance. If we're married, they cannot do anything. Get dressed, Gisela. Make yourself presentable. I'll be back in two hours."

He stepped outside but didn't go far, judging by the bellowing of his voice as he argued with another man.

"Who's there, Thebe?" Gisela moved over to peek out the door over Thebe's shoulder.

"The sheriff from Cromarty."

Donald's voice carried to them clearly. "I'm getting the priest now. We'll be married by nightfall."

The sheriff answered, though Gisela struggled to hear him. "You'd better. There's naught more I can do to help you. I want the coin you promised me."

Donald stormed back inside, sending the two of them scampering away from the door, grabbed a small bag hidden in a cupboard, then returned to the sheriff. "More than your help was worth. Get ye gone."

"Are you sure 'tis all here? I have to leave before they arrive. I cannot be seen with you."

"'Tis all you're getting. Now get out of my sight."

The other man strode up to Donald until his face was less than a hand's length from his. "I'll not be helping you anymore. You don't know how to control yourself, MacKinnie."

Then he mounted and rode off. Donald flung himself onto his own mount and followed a moment later.

Gisela knew this was her last chance. "Thebe, please let me go."

"Nay, I'll not." She snatched up a mallet from the table and held it over her head. "I'll split your skull and tell him you fell. He'll kill me if you're not here when he returns."

Gisela had to take a chance. She was younger and stronger than the maid, and she wouldn't have hesitated, if not for the hammer. She leaped on Thebe, and they fell to the floor together, a writhing knot of anger and desperation. Gisela fought for the hammer, wrestling it out of her hands.

Gisela ran, and the other woman chased after her with a roar of desperation. Back into the woods she went, carrying the hammer with her.

She glanced over her shoulder, and a lump formed in her throat. Thebe had grabbed a small sword and was headed straight for her, her eyes wild with hate, a madness there Gisela had never seen before. She ducked behind a clump of trees, trying desperately to calm her breathing so her gasping wouldn't give her away as she waited for Thebe to draw even with her. As the lass's face came into view, Gisela leaped at her from the side, as good as throwing the mallet in her rush to knock her to the ground. The hammer flew right past the maid, bouncing into the undergrowth, as they sprawled in the leaves and sticks of the forest floor.

Thebe lay motionless beneath her, not even a sound after the whuff that left her as they hit the ground. Gisela pushed herself away from the woman, trying to make sense of what had happened. Dark red blood spread across the woman's gown. She rolled Thebe to her back and gasped. The sword protruded from her belly.

Thebe looked at her in shock, her mouth trying to form words, but pink froth came from her lips, gurgling in an odd way. The glassy look in Thebe's eyes told Gisela the lass was leaving this world. Gisela whimpered as she watched the light of life fade.

She was dead.

Pushing herself to her feet, Gisela panted with fear. She'd just killed a woman who worked for her clan. Someone was dead because of her. Reminding herself that she'd had to defend herself didn't ease her guilt. She twisted the fabric of her dirty gown in her hand, pulling it tight until she let out a small scream.

Frantic, she whirled in a circle, her gaze searching for Donald or his accomplice, but she saw no one. Fighting to push the sobs back deep inside her so they would not erupt, she forced herself to stop and think. She needed to move quickly. A horse.

She returned to the cottage, reminding herself that she'd seen Donald ride away only minutes ago. In a lean-to behind the house, she found a smaller mount, presumably Thebe's.

She needed a weapon, but she would not, could not go back to Thebe's body and retrieve the sword. Instead, she searched the cottage, eventually finding a small dagger in a sheath she could fasten to her belt.

Mounting quickly, she followed the path Donald and the sheriff had taken, hoping it would take her toward the coastline. She needed to find her bearings before Donald returned. Though the risk was higher, the open path would be faster on horseback than going through the woods. Distance was her priority now.

After about an hour, she finally hit the shoreline, the smell of the firth telling her where she was. She stopped at the edge of the forest, ignoring the midgies that plagued her and tried to determine how far down the coast she was and exactly how far she'd have to travel to reach Matheson land.

She hadn't gone far when the sound of horse hooves carried to her, so she led her horse further under the trees, praying that whoever it was wouldn't be able to see her. She held her breath, nearly losing it when the horse went on by her. Donald.

But he didn't stop, and her breath came out in

a whoosh.

Her horse seemed to share her relief, or perhaps it was happy to see its stablemate. It let out a nicker, and Gisela squeaked in surprise. Donald stopped. Her heart hammered against her ribcage as she watched him scan the area, taking his time to take in everything in the forest, giving little attention to the coastline of the firth a short distance away.

She should have jumped in and swam to her brothers. He'd have never caught her then.

After what seemed eternal suspense, he finally turned back to the front and picked up the reins of his horse.

But her horse betrayed her again with another snort.

He whipped his head around, then turned fully, finding his way back toward her. His gaze searched the ground, then the trees again, and she swore her trembling body would give her away.

He broke into a wide smile. "There you are, my love."

He'd found her.

CHAPTER EIGHTEEN

———◆———

PADRAIG AND TORCALL left in the morn with over a hundred warriors, moving steadily toward Black Isle. He had plenty of time to think on his life as they rode.

His mind went to John de Bethune, someone he'd never forget and hoped to see again. Though he'd been sad to see him go, the surgeon had said he had many things to accomplish yet, so he would return to London to learn more about healing, a choice made to prevent his arrest again in the Highlands.

Padraig had the sudden inkling to do the same—get on with his life. Find Gisela, propose and marry her, find a way the two could work together as healers. Have bairns of their own. The possibilities were endless. If she agreed, he wasn't ready to travel the country just yet, not under the circumstances.

A band of a hundred men and horses moved more slowly than a single man alone, and they stopped as nightfall approached. Inverness lay only a few miles distant, telling them Black Isle was not far.

Padraig turned to Torcall, who rode beside him as a guide. "What say you from here?"

"Since 'tis nearly dusk, I say we take a small group into Inverness and find out what is happening with the clans on Black Isle. They'll know at any inn or tavern. Word of Donald and his crimes has traveled. Especially since he left his sire. Everyone knows the MacKinnie chief is searching for him. And they've all heard about Dagga and Gisella. There'll be many tongues wagging in the burgh."

Padraig and Torcall crossed the camp to his cousin Connor. "Torcall and I are heading into Inverness to get what information we can about the current state of affairs on Black Isle."

"Once we're certain of alliances and the movements, we can make our plans more effectively," Torcall said.

Connor nodded in agreement. "The moon is bright tonight, so it could be the best time for an attack. I'm happy to take our hundred against MacKinnie's two hundred or even three hundred with his allies. Men who don't fight for their own clan are easier to take down. Each of our men can take down three of theirs," he said with a smirk, the ever-present Grant confidence dancing across his face.

Padraig felt a sudden pride when Torcall looked at him with his brow arched in question. "Truly?"

Connor chuckled. "Truly. Find out their number and where they are. I'll be happy to lead our men on."

"We can gain another three score at Matheson

land."

"Clan MacKinnie is farther north than Eddirdale?"

"Aye, farther across the isle, about an hour more."

"How long to go to Inverness and back?"

"An hour for the journey and return, plus the time we're there gathering the latest news."

"Perfect. We'll catch a quick sleep and be ready to fight around midnight."

"I'll wake you on our return," Padraig said.

Connor laughed. "Not necessary. I'll hear you." He shouted toward a cluster of men, and a group of ten broke off, mounted up again, and rode over. "In case of trouble," he said with a wink for his cousin.

Padraig shook his head in amusement, chuckled, and turned his horse toward Inverness. Behind him, Connor barked instructions to the men remaining in camp.

They rode in silence to Inverness, and once in the city, Torcall led them to a busy inn. Padraig sent six men off to the center of town just to talk to any of the city's men who were still out and about seeking wine or companions from the nearest brothel, while he followed Torcall inside, leaving the other four out front.

"Torcall!" Someone called out as soon as they entered. The Matheson guard headed straight over to the man and his table of companions. Padraig didn't recognize him, but their welcome was warm enough. "What the hell are you doing here? I hear Clan Matheson is about to be attacked. Could it be true?"

"What? I just left there two days ago. What's this news now?"

"They say that MacKinnie has Marcas's sister held captive, but Matheson is holding the priest. Chief MacKinnie has offered generous coin to anyone willing to fight with him. Heard he's calling on Clan Milton for their assistance."

Torcall swore under his breath. "My thanks to you, MacHeth. Will you fight with us? We cannot allow Gisela to come to harm at the hands of a madman."

"'Tis why I'm here. I'm bringing more to support you. We'll be there on the morrow."

"Do you know how many MacKinnie has?"

"They say he could be at fifty more than their two hundred already. You'll need help, after the way the curse depleted your ranks." The other men at the table were all listening closely, taking in all they said.

Padraig spoke up. "We brought help, though nowhere near two hundred. We have five score Grant warriors, and more will be coming soon. We're grateful to have you at our backs. Where are they holding Gisela?"

"Last we heard, Donald had her in hiding but was planning to bring her to MacKinnie Castle for the wedding."

"Wedding!" Torcall cursed. "There'll be no wedding."

"She could be married by now if they managed to get the priest off Matheson land."

Padraig nodded to the men. "Many thanks to

you all, but I can see we have no time to waste."

Torcall thanked the men and followed him out. The other men were gathering, and Padraig asked, "Did you hear anything?"

All of them had heard the same news that Padraig and Torcall had gathered. One man added, "Most are guessing MacKinnie will attack Eddirdale on the morrow. Donald wishes to get the priest, and he'll do whatever he must."

Padraig nodded, his lips pursed. Images of Gisela held captive, tied up, in Donald's arms raced through his mind. But the worst thought— he couldn't stop it from blooming brighter in his mind, like the light of a white rose under a summer moon.

He could be too late. She could be Donald's wife already.

———————◆———————

Donald grabbed the reins of Gisela's horse with a whoop. "You're a stubborn one, aren't you, lass. And I'll never let you go. I don't know how you managed to get away from Thebe. She would fight the devil just to please me, but I'll not need her around when I bed you." He waggled his brow at her. "I may keep her around after we marry. 'Twill be good to have a biddable lass in my bed." He slowed his horse and leaned over to lift her onto his own mount. She did her best to push him away, but he considered it a game, and after all she'd been through, her strength was waning.

Gisela kept quiet. She wasn't about to tell him what really happened to Thebe.

Donald gave her an odd look, then spurred his horse in the direction she'd just come from. Turning her mind to constant prayer, she ignored everything Donald said, keeping her back as straight as possible to keep from touching the bastard.

But he rambled constantly, and his voice drilled into her, whether she wanted it to or not.

"You'll be happy. You'll see, Gisela. I'll take good care of you. You're the only one for me. 'Tis destiny. 'Twas what my sire said long ago. The moment I met you, I knew we were meant to spend our lives together. We'll have a dozen handsome sons. Och, I suppose you'll want a lass or two, so we may have four and ten by the time we're done. I'll have a wing built onto the castle just for us. A new tower. 'Tis exactly what we'll need. I'll have it started as soon as we marry."

Gisela closed her eyes and prayed for patience and Padraig. Why had she denied her handsome Grant? She loved Padraig with all her heart. After all she'd been through, she knew she would follow Padraig wherever he wished to go. Perhaps they could agree to split their time. Half the year traveling and half the year on Matheson land.

As much as she loved her wee niece and nephew, she knew she'd never be satisfied without Padraig in her life. And Kara and Tiernay had come to love and trust Brigid sooner even than she had expected. At first, it had hurt her feelings to see them turning toward the newcomer rather than herself, but now she realized it was the best thing for the two bairns. Marcas adored Brigid, and their family would find a deep happiness together that Marcas never could have had with Freda. Marcas and Brigid had shown her what love looked like, and she wanted that with Padraig. Only Padraig.

"Donald, please. You don't love me, and I don't love you. Please let me go. We have grown apart, and I don't wish to ever leave my brother."

"Nonsense. You are my property and you will learn to love me." He let go of the horse's reins with one hand, and Gisela turned to see what he did. Would he hit her? But no. His hand went to his head and held it. His expression pinched, as if he were in pain.

"What's wrong, Donald?"

"Naught. My head pains me sometimes. Especially when you talk of leaving me." He rubbed his head with his knuckles. Hard. As if punishing himself would make his problems disappear.

"Donald, I love another. I didn't know it before, but now I do."

"How can you love another when I am here for you? I am the best for you. Destiny says so." He closed his eyes and nearly steered his horse into a tree, her horse being forced to follow. The lead horse swerved at the last minute, but her horse had nowhere to go.

"Watch out!" Gisela yelled. She covered her face with her hands and tipped to the side, doing what she could to prevent scraping against the tree as they brushed past it too close for comfort.

Donald jerked the horse onto the correct path, and it snorted in protest of the rough handling.

"Donald, if you truly love me, you'll want me to be happy. My heart aches for him. He has the nicest smile, and he makes me laugh."

"I can make you laugh, and once we are married, I'll smile more."

He gave her an emphatic nod, then whimpered a low, "Och." His knuckles returned to the side of his head.

She longed for Padraig. No one else had the lighthearted outlook he did, the fun-loving attitude, a way of bringing bubbling laughter out of her at the oddest moments. Could she make Donald see the differences between them? "But will you make me giggle when you try to toss me into the firth? Or stand outside my window and sing me a song—a silly one with foolish words? Or will you rub my back until I forget all my troubles and fall asleep?" She thought of all the reasons she loved Padraig, about his smile and his loving ways, about how his stories from his travels made her chuckle.

About how whenever she looked at him, she could see his feelings for her all over his face.

Padraig loved her. She needed his humor, sure, and his lightness after the dark days of the curse. But in this moment, she needed his strong arms and fierce loyalty.

"You'll forget him after he's gone."

"But he won't be gone, I tell you."

"He will. I'll make sure of it." The scowl on his face convinced her he meant it.

She swung her arm out and barely caught his shoulder. "Why? Why would you hurt an innocent man?"

He grabbed her hand and said, "Stop. I haven't hurt him. I just said you'll never see him again after we're married."

"What do you mean? How could you do that?" She had no idea what his riddles and teases meant.

"I'll make certain that he's in jail, and he'll never get out. He'll never be found, not until it's too late for him to come to you."

Gisela nearly heaved over the side of the horse. Hopeless. This entire situation was hopeless. She gave up trying to convince Donald to let her go. He had an answer for her every argument, even if they only made sense in his own head. But she would never marry him—even if Padraig was lost to her.

They arrived at MacKinnie Castle, and the guards opened the gates, closing them again as soon as they were through. One of them gave a quick bow of his head and said, "Your sire wishes to see you inside his solar. You're to take her with you."

Donald helped her down from his horse, then led her into the keep, one hand clamped around her wrist, his other still rubbing his head. As soon as they stepped into the great hall, every conversation echoing around the space fell silent, and every pair of eyes fastened on them as they walked up the staircase to the solar.

As they entered, Chief MacKinnie stood, his arms waving wildly. "What in God's name are you doing, Donald? You'll cause the ruin of our clan, our legacy, destroy everything we have built.

You're making so many enemies, I'll never be able to find enough warriors to defend our holdings. We're lucky a few Miltons are willing to honor our alliance. You cannot steal a priest!"

"I don't intend to steal him. If we can kill half the Mathesons, they'll surely give him up. Once the wedding is done, everything will be right again. Why are you worried, Da? You are the mightiest of all. You and me. We always have been."

"Why am I worried? Because the Mathesons have strong allies. Ramsay archers who can shoot you between the eyes. Grants who wield swords like demons. Do you never listen to all the tales about their battles? If either clan comes to the Mathesons' aid, 'twill be the end of us. Only your brother will survive, and only because he's gone into hiding."

"Well, the Ramsays are not coming."

His father fell into his chair with a deep sigh. "Thank the Lord above."

"The Grants are coming."

His father bolted out of his chair again. "The Grants? God's blood, Donald. Nay! 'Tis worse than the Ramsays. Give her to me. I'll keep her safe in my solar. If anything happens to her, it'll be the end of our clan."

Donald pushed her behind his back. "No one touches her but me, Da. I'm going to tie her up somewhere, and no one will know where but me. If they don't bring the priest, I'll drive a stake through her heart."

CHAPTER NINETEEN

———————•◆•———————

T HE GRANT WARRIORS arrived at Eddirdale Castle shortly after midnight. Padraig waved to Ethan on the curtain wall and called, "Open the gate, Ethan. I need to speak with Marcas."

The gate clanked open for Padraig, and Connor gave his men a brief respite outside the wall. "Be ready to mount up again at a moment's notice," he ordered before stepping to Padraig's side.

Padraig, Connor, and Torcall greeted the Matheson brothers and Alvery, clasping arms with each of them in turn.

"What's the current situation? We've heard all kinds of tales," Padraig said, clenching his hands into fists to control his impatience. He needed to make plans with his allies, not go haring off on his own.

"Donald has Gisela, but we don't know where," Shaw said. "We found Thebe dead, a sword in her belly, not far from a cottage. It looks like someone was tied to the bed at the cottage, probably Gisela, but we don't know where either she or Donald are."

"Has there been any sign of a sheriff from Cromarty?" Padraig asked, giving a quick summary of the story of his false arrest.

"Aye," Marcas said. "One of my men spotted him this afternoon, riding as if all the demons of hell were after him. He's known to take gold to lock up an innocent man and forget about him for a few months. You're lucky you were only there a few days."

Indeed, Padraig counted his blessings. But he forced the memory and his anger at the sheriff aside. "We'll deal with him later. Now we need to focus on Gisela. Where is the priest? Please tell me he's safe." Padraig ran his hand through his hair, wanting so badly to act, but he couldn't yet. He had to find out exactly how things lay.

Running blindly would do him no good.

"We have the priest in our hall, and he has agreed to stay," Shaw said. "He wants no part of MacKinnie forcing a marriage on Gisela, and he refuses to leave until this is finished. He's afraid of both Donald and his sire." He crossed his arms and shrugged. "Cannot blame the poor man. He's as nervous as a criminal at his own hanging."

"Let's work out a plan, then. I'm ready to go, and we have men outside who are ready to fight. What about you? How many Mathesons will join us?"

"Shaw and I will go with you," Marcas said. "Ethan will stay to protect the castle. We'll bring two score and leave a score here with Ethan and the women. We're guessing MacKinnie to have two hundred of his own, plus a score from

Milton's, maybe another score have signed on for the extra coin he's been offering. Can you work with those numbers, Connor?" Marcas was standing strong, but Padraig noticed Brigid, Jennet, and Tara standing together on the keep steps, listening closely as they laid their plans for battle.

"Aye, we Grants will sweep through them like they were the Norse at Largs, send them running to hide," Connor said. "Padraig, are you ready? It's time to end this and get your lass back. Ethan, if this is a trick on their part to draw us out so they can attack the castle, send word, and we'll be back as quickly as possible. But I don't think they'll be foolish enough to come here and leave their own castle undefended from a force of charging Grants." He started to walk away, but then spun around to say, "How could I forget? My brother has at least another hundred warriors coming along behind us by half a day. They'll support you, as well."

"Wonderful, many thanks to you," Marcas said. "We'll be with you in a moment." He and Ethan stepped away from the group to speak with Brigid and Jennet, each man drawing close to his woman. Shaw followed Connor out the gates to where the Grant warriors checked equipment and tended their stamping horses.

Padraig followed Marcas and Ethan, looking at the three faces of Brigid and his beloved cousins. While they remained strong, worry still etched their faces. "We'll get her back. I promise. We have plenty of Grant warriors, and more coming soon."

Marcas kissed Brigid's cheek, then wrapped his arms around her in a lingering embrace.

Brigid said, "Please bring her home safely. We fear for her and miss her desperately. Godspeed to all of you."

Ethan gave Jennet a quick hug. "I'll protect you all. We'll hold the castle, should MacKinnie try anything."

Padraig and Marcas walked across the courtyard together to join Connor and Shaw. It was time.

He would not return without Gisela.

And if the priest was still here, he'd marry her.

———— ♦ ————

Gisela looked out toward the gates of the MacKinnie curtain wall. She was tied up inside some building inside the curtain wall of MacKinnie Castle, sacks of grain and other stores all around her. He'd stuck a disgusting, smelly old cloth in her mouth to keep her from yelling, then kissed her cheek with a smile. "I'll be back soon, my love."

He'd left her exactly where no one would think to look. Noble hostages and captives would normally be hidden in the cellar of the keep or behind a locked door abovestairs, not out with the mice. If there were to be a battle, she was in the worst possible place—too close to the fighting, but unable to see what transpired. Her only light was from a torch lit on the curtain wall, and there was one window at the top of the building. Even if she were free she wasn't tall enough to look out.

But it gave her a touch of light in the dark.

Initially, she'd thought Donald was acting on his own, but she'd paid close attention to all that happened around her and seen that he had more support than she'd imagined. His father had vowed to assist him in seeing this marriage come to fruition. She'd counted the warriors she'd seen around MacKinnie Castle, both inside the bailey and outside the curtain wall. A number of warriors who'd come to help MacKinnie wore no plaid, no identification. She knew exactly what that meant—they'd come for the promise of coin and did not care a bit about her fate or who was in the right. And she knew how many warriors Clan Matheson had, or how few rather, thanks to the curse. They would be sorely outnumbered.

She prayed for help for her clan.

Were the Grants truly on their way? She prayed they were. She wished to be away from Donald forever, but more than that, she wished for safety for her brothers and her clan. She nearly began to cry, but since her nose would run and she was unable to wipe it, she thought it better to keep her tears at bay.

She needed to stay strong for Padraig. The Grants were coming.

The only thing she could do was pray.

CHAPTER TWENTY

THE MATHESON AND Grant forces arrived outside MacKinnie Castle in less than two hours, the light of the moon helping speed their travel. The parapets were lined with archers and men with swords. They were expected, clearly. Padraig was surprised at the number of archers—he hadn't known the MacKinnies to train much in archery.

He couldn't help but wonder how skilled they were.

Marcas shouted to the men at the gates. "I've come for my sister."

"She's not here," a guard yelled back.

"The hell she isn't, you lying bastards. If we have to take down your walls stone by stone to find her, we will."

A new face appeared at the top of the curtain wall, next to the gates.

Donald.

Connor whispered to Marcas. "Keep him talking. I have a few men who can come over the wall in the back. They'll move quickly and quietly, take out who they must to prevent anyone sounding the alarm, then open the gates to allow us entrance. We'll settle this quickly."

Marcas gave a small nod to Connor, which also effectively hid his smirk from Donald. The Grant commander made a subtle motion with his hand, and a small group of men at the back of the line rode quietly away.

To the MacKinnies, it would look like they were leaving.

Donald pumped his fist over his head. "I want the priest. Get him here so this can be finished. You'll never find Gisela without me. You have no choice but to withdraw and bring the priest."

"Never!" Marcas yelled. "My sister will never be yours."

"I wouldn't fight if I were you, Matheson. Half your men have turned to run." Donald nodded toward the back of their group, but neither Connor nor Marcas gave any indication they heard him. "Took one look at all our archers and showed their true cowardice."

Little did he know that Alex Grant and his brothers had spent a great deal of time training certain warriors with quick minds in stealth, strategy, and navigation, even through castles they'd never seen before. They scaled trees or used ropes or simply climbed if the wall offered sufficient hand and footholds to breach a castle's curtain wall. Once inside, their goal was to reach the gatehouse. With knives at their throats, the guards at the gate were more than willing to do as they were told—keep quiet while the Grant men set to work.

The gate would come up before the castle guards understood why. The distraction and surprise was almost as helpful in an attack as the gate opening.

"We'll kill all your men if that's what it takes, MacKinnie!" Shaw bellowed. "Are you sure your sire wishes for that to happen?"

"'Twas my sire who hired fifty men to fight with us. That gives us more than two hundred. You and your measly crew will be dead in moments. Then we'll march down and take your castle. We should have done it in the middle of the curse."

Connor spurred his mount forward, his horse's chain mail jingling as if eager for the coming battle. Connor was fully outfitted himself, with a chest plate for added protection.

"Surrender now, MacKinnie. I have a hundred Grant warriors who will trample your force before they land a single blow. Ye've heard of the Grants' skill in battle, I'm sure. None can stand against us."

Padraig did his best to hide his smile. How the Grants loved to boast about their skills, though he'd yet to hear Connor say anything that wasn't the absolute truth.

"We'll wait and see," Donald replied. "You have half the hour to produce the priest, and then our archers will start shooting."

Marcas shrugged. "Even if we agree to bring the priest, Donald, you must give us more time," he said, allowing Donald to think Marcas would surrender to his demands. "You know we cannot get to Matheson land and return within such a short time. Three hours, no less."

Padraig noticed a flash from one of the narrow, slitted windows at the top of the gatehouse and knew it to be the signal from one of the covert warriors inside the castle. The next moment, his cousin's hand lifted, he let out his Grant war whoop, and the gate lifted, opening from the inside.

They charged.

Padraig swung his sword at the first opponent he reached, catching the man's arm and tossing him from his horse. Out of the corner of his eye, he saw two archers tumbling off the curtain wall, killed either by their men inside or the Grant archers.

He fought his way through the MacKinnie forces and through the gate. Men gave way before the Grant assault like autumn leaves in a storm—swirling, flying, ultimately falling to the ground. He lost track of how many blows he dealt, how many fell under his horse's hooves. Finally he paused in a gap in the battle to catch his breath, and looking up, he noticed Donald on top of the curtain wall, well out of the melee. And he'd spoken of cowardice.

Connor seemed to see him at the same time, and the two Grants shared a look. Which of them would take Donald? Padraig nodded. He wanted him. Donald was his for daring to touch Gisela and for the harm he'd done to innocents in his quest to punish Padraig. But he needed to be careful, because it was possible that only Donald knew where she was.

Connor gave a quick salute and went back on the offensive. His warhorse, black as midnight, reared up on its hind legs and took three men out with that one move, sending another half dozen running, the yells of the wounded echoing across the landscape.

Connor grinned madly as he went about his bloody work.

Padraig couldn't help but watch his cousin in all his splendor. Connor fought as if he considered his sword to be a part of him, so deadly, yet with a mesmerizing grace. He sometimes seemed to toy with his opponents, knocking men off their steeds and allowing them to survive.

But if they were foolish enough to return and try to sink their weapons into his flesh, Connor gave no quarter.

Then the battle rose up around Padraig again, and he plunged back into the fray. When next he looked up, he noticed they'd either taken out or beaten back most of the mounted men. Riderless horses whinnied in fear and sought to escape the roiling courtyard. Donald still stood on the wall, bellowing at his men. It was time for Padraig to act. He turned his horse toward the stairs to the top of the wall and made his way through the courtyard, beating off any who stood in his way. When he could ride no further, he slid to the ground and took the last three steps to the stair. Five men guarded his path up.

Connor appeared at his side. "I'll go with you. Do not deny me the pleasure."

Padraig nodded with a grim smile, glad of his cousin's support. Two men fell swiftly beneath their swords. The last three ran up the stair, going not toward Donald to protect him, but the opposite direction. He had to chuckle. Connor shot him a grin and a salute before returning to the battle in the courtyard.

Padraig made a slow ascent, and two Grant warriors took his place at the base of the stair to guard his back.

Now it was just Padraig and Donald.

Donald roared wordlessly when he saw Padraig, then took a step back. "Grant, you should be in Hell! I paid good money to get rid of you." Then both his hands went to his head. He bent at the waist and roared again, this time seemingly more in pain than anger.

"Arm yourself, Donald," he called out, ignoring the man's posture. Whether his pain was real or not, he didn't care. He had to find Gisela. "You'll never have Gisela. She is mine."

Donald finally drew his sword, a small thing, and swung it wildly with one hand while the other rubbed the side of his head. Something was clearly wrong with the man, the growth John had suggested or something else. Donald seemed suddenly possessed, flailing wildly in no one direction. It wasn't out of the realm of possibility that Donald could die before his very eyes, without his ever landing a blow. He had to find out where Gisela was before Donald died, by his hand or whatever ate at his brain.

Donald straightened and stopped his wild

slashing. "You'll never have her because you'll never find her, Grant. I'm the only one who can find her."

Padraig had him cornered. Donald pressed his back against the parapet, and Padraig could take a single step and plunge his sword deep into the man's bowels or sever his neck with one swing. But he couldn't do it. Not yet. He caught sight of Marcas in the middle of the courtyard. "Matheson, have you found your sister yet?" he bellowed.

One word from Marcas, the right word, and he would be free to kill the bastard in front of him.

"Nay, she's not inside the keep. We've searched everywhere."

Donald began to chuckle. He dropped the hand from his head, his laughter bubbling out of his mouth in a cascade of madness unlike anything Padraig had ever heard.

Kill him, kill him.

But Donald's weapon hung at his side, and he made no move to attack Padraig. And he still had no idea where Gisela was.

Donald had him by the bollocks, and he knew it, glee and triumph dancing across his face as though God himself had just placed a crown on his head. "I'm the only one who will have her!" Donald erupted into a chilling laugh that carried over the landscape of Black Isle.

He was a true scourge over the land.

And Padraig couldn't kill him.

CHAPTER TWENTY-ONE

———◆———

GISELA DID HER best to free herself from her bindings, but Donald had tied them too tightly, her tender skin tearing from the coarse rope. She knew exactly when the Matheson warriors had arrived, could hear the shouting at the gates, but she couldn't understand their words.

But she did understand the war whoop. And it was not the Matheson nor the MacKinnie whoop that rang out first, so she guessed, prayed the Grants had come and it was their battle cry she heard.

Padraig was here, a wee string in her heart tugged to tell her so, and he'd brought help. She had to believe, no matter what evil plan Donald had initiated for Padraig, he was intelligent enough to get himself out of it, especially with all the support he could rally.

Of course, the proof of that was in reasoning. If a band of Grant warriors were here, Padraig had brought them. That meant only one thing.

Donald was home again out of fear.

He'd locked her inside his castle because he was afraid. Otherwise, she'd still be tied to the bed in the cottage, Thebe or not.

She swore she heard Padraig's voice amongst the clamor of shouts and cries. Tears misted her vision, but she forced them away, staring up at the roof and chewing on the wretched gag Donald had stuffed in her mouth. But what good was loosening her gag if she couldn't free her hands or her feet?

Someone might hear her if she screamed, even through the sounds of battle. Even though she was hidden in some building. Eventually, the battle would end, and if the Mathesons and Grants triumphed, they would be searching for her. She had to be prepared.

She envisioned the rescuing force of warriors taking over the castle, her brothers and Padraig searching everywhere inside the keep, expecting to find her in a bedchamber or in the great hall, only to be disappointed.

Donald had been careful to keep anyone from seeing where he'd brought her, this storage building tucked into a corner. She cursed at the bugs crawling all about her, the cold, hard floor she sat on, and the dimness of the space.

Chewing at the disgusting rag tied across her mouth, she nearly wept. It was two or three layers thick, impossible to chew through. She wanted to scream from the frustration raking through her, and if she could scratch, kick, or yell, she would do all three together just because she knew it would feel wonderful. If the bastard stood in front of her and she were unbound, he'd feel the wrath of her entire being.

But Donald had made sure she was completely helpless. She was at his mercy.

Then the worst happened. Her gaze caught something moving, a slow, sinuous motion.

Her biggest fear.

The one thing that could make her scream, cry, and sob all at once.

She fought her gag, tugging, pulling with her chin and tongue, making the oddest shapes she could with her mouth in a wild attempt to bring it to one thickness she could chew through just because the sight of her enemy was more than she could bear. Oblivious to her presence, it continued its trek through the building.

The dreaded adder.

The snake slithered from its meal behind the grain, probably feeding on some rodent drawn by the grain. Gray in color with a zig-zag design on its back, it was the movement of the pattern on the ground that caught her eye, even in the dark of the night. It entered a spot where the torchlight reflected off its back, bringing her strength she didn't know she had, the panic that coursed through her reaching a level that would cause her whole insides to burst if she didn't free herself soon.

Struggling with her ties, biting at the cloth in her mouth, she reminded herself how her father had told her over and over again that the snake's venom wasn't strong enough to kill a human, and that the snake was more afraid of her than she was of it.

She found that hard to believe. In fact, she was

extremely close to wetting herself.

If she left it alone, it would not bother her.

How she wished the man stood in front of her now, so she could give him a piece of her mind about the evils of snakes, no matter how shy they were. And then he could save her. But she was alone, no one to save her but herself. She was not about to get the attention of the creature crawling across the stone of the granary, oblivious to her presence. If it had noticed her, it would have surely gone the other way.

It came closer…

And closer…

A scream erupted from deep inside her, one that would curl anyone's toes, make anyone with a sound mind run in the other direction. And once she started, she couldn't stop. Not because of the snake. Because of everything—Donald and Thebe and Padraig and being tied to a bed and inside a building and missing her father and mother and the sounds of battle and dying men ringing in her ears.

She screamed and screamed and screamed.

———— ◆ ————

Padraig froze, lifting his head in the warm night breeze. He heard something. A sound so full of fear that he guessed it could only be one person.

Gisela.

The scream carried to them so clearly, so powerfully, that if Donald weren't standing in front of him with the same strange look on his face that Padraig was sure was on his own, he would have guessed that the man was pulling her fingernails out one by one.

Donald turned to him with a roar, raising his weapon, but Padraig moved before he could strike. He plunged his sword into Donald's thigh—he needed the brute alive—before yanking it out just as quickly. Donald dropped his sword, grabbing the bleeding wound as he stared at Padraig in disbelief. As quickly as his hands had gone to his leg, they returned to his head with a roar, a look of sheer pain crossing his features. Padraig, not sure what would happen next, took a step back and held his sword low and ready, pointed at the man's gut. Donald's gaze fastened on him, and he reached for Padraig's throat, mindless of the sword between them. Padraig held fast, and Donald ran himself onto Padraig's sword. It sank into his belly before the bastard could complete his mission. Even then, Donald didn't seem to notice. He clawed at his head again, and a peacefulness crossed his face. Then he toppled, slid free of Padraig's sword, and down, off the curtain wall to certain death on the ground outside the castle.

Padraig held onto his weapon and leapt down the stairs, another scream carrying to him as he ran, this one from outside the castle wall, rather than inside like the first. He quickly cleaned his sword on the grass and returned it to its sheath, then mounted his horse in one swift move and raced toward the source of the scream.

He passed Marcas and Shaw, both riding hard in the same direction, but Padraig's big warhorse had extra speed this night, sensing the urgency of his rider.

"If you find her, take her back to Matheson land," Marcas called out after him.

"Get her the hell away from here, Grant!" Shaw shouted.

Padraig raised a hand to let them know he'd heard, then continued on, wishing Gisela would scream one more time. He had visions of wildcats and wolves, any creature in the middle of the night, attacking his sweet lass. Some feral beast chasing her through the trees.

Her sobs carried to him, and he followed, his horse crashing through the forest like a red deer running from a hound. He reined in when he hit a path and listened. Riding directionless would serve him no good.

And good thing he had, too. The cries reached him from his right, away from MacKinnie land. He was close. He urged Midnight Blue into a ground-eating trot—fast enough to catch up to her, slow enough that he wouldn't race right by.

Thunder sounded close by, drowning out her sobs, but he caught sight of her in a dead run away from him. "Gisela! Turn around!"

Gisela, still crying, turned around, her face contorted in fear.

"Arms up, lass! Stand still."

She spun around and stepped off to the side of the path, staring at him for a moment before breaking into a wide smile. She lifted her arms up to him. He slowed his horse and he leaned down, scooping her up around the waist and tossing her onto his lap, a move all the Grant youth had practiced after their Uncle Brodie had saved Aunt Celestina the same way.

She fell against him, her arms wrapping tight around his waist. Her grip on him told him just how frightened she was. He kissed her forehead, then chuckled. "Careful, lass. You'll knock me off the horse. Or is that your intent? Your brothers are not far behind me, so we probably should not make love just yet. I don't think they'd approve." He hoped his jesting would ease her mind.

She loosened her arms a little and pressed her face into his chest, mumbling words he couldn't make out. He slowed his horse, pushed her back a wee bit and lifted her chin to give her a kiss on the lips. "I love you, Gisela. Stop your worry. Donald will never bother you again."

"Snake."

He chortled. "What?"

"I love you, too, Padraig. Snake. Blasted snake was trying to kill me."

"An adder? Did it bite you?"

"Nay," she mumbled, letting out another sob.

"Then how did it try to kill you?"

"Nearly scared me to death…"

He laughed. "And you the bravest lass I know. Gisela, will you marry me?"

"Aye, please. I never should have turned you down. You're the only one for me." Then she paused for a moment, holding her breath to listen to the sounds around them. "Thunder. A thunderstorm. That is just what we need this night. Please take me away, anywhere, far away before I become addled."

"That beautiful sound is not thunder." Padraig heard it more clearly now and recognized it. "'Tis the Grant cavalry coming to assist us. They'll help your brother break the last of the MacKinnie defense."

They reached the main road that led to MacKinnie Castle, so he stopped Midnight Blue back from the crossing just as the Grant warriors thundered past them, a sight that always impressed him, no matter how often he saw it. One rider peeled off and circled back to them.

"Padraig! You are hale? Is that Gisela? You've found her?"

He was truly relieved to see his sire. "Aye, we're well. Connor and Marcas could use a wee bit of help mopping up, but I'm taking her to Matheson land. Orders from her brothers. Gisela, meet my father, Robbie Grant."

She shifted in his lap and ducked her head. "'Tis a pleasure, my lord. Please forgive my appearance."

His father laughed and said, "Nice to finally meet you, lass." Then he looked at his son. "Get her to safety. I'll tell her brothers you've found her. We'll see you in a wee bit."

Padraig waited until the horsemen had passed before moving on, his many comrades sending hoots, whoops, and cheers his way as they saw Gisela plastered firmly against him.

He knew he should take her inside the Matheson keep, but instead whispered to her, "Gisela, will you handfast with me?"

"Aye, please," she said, her eyes searching his

face. "I wish to go to our cottage behind the village, just the two of us. I cannot marry until Marcas and Shaw are back. But please take me away now, somewhere we can be alone."

"Patience, lass." Padraig saw his sire still waiting to join the group and called out to him. "Da! Will you do us the honor of witnessing our handfasting?"

His father smiled, turning his horse back to face them and coming abreast of them. "'Twould be my honor." He reached into his saddlebag and pulled out another Grant plaid. "These are special circumstances. 'Twon't require much." He held out the strip of plaid and waited.

Padraig took hold of Gisela's hand, clasping hers with his, then reached for the plaid and wrapped it around their hands.

His father said, "Do you pledge your troth to each other once a priest can be found? Gisela?"

She stared at Padraig with so much love in her gaze that it humbled him. "Aye."

"Padraig. Do you pledge your troth to Gisela?"

"Aye." He'd never meant anything as much as that one word he spoke.

"Consider yourselves handfasted. Now get her to safety," he said, pulling the plaid back up and rolling it. "Welcome to Clan Grant, lass." Then he smiled and joined the line of horses headed toward MacKinnie land.

"I've never been happier, husband. Take me away."

Padraig kissed her briefly and tugged on the reins, sending them off toward Matheson land.

When they reached Eddirdale Castle, they rode right past it and through the village until they found the hut they'd shared after Jennet's rescue from the witchery trial. He swung off his horse, then scooped her into his arms and carried her inside, closing the door with a kick. He set her on her feet in the silvery moonlight coming through a window and got to work shucking his clothes.

Gisela watched him, wide eyed. "I love you, Padraig. I missed you so much, and I need you more than anything. Please."

Padraig moaned, taking her lips with his and devouring her.

CHAPTER TWENTY-TWO

———————◆———————

GISELA SIGHED AS Padraig kissed her, and she pulled at her ribbons—with his help—to drop her gown to the floor, shoving it away from her with a shudder.

"Padraig, I've waited for you." Tearing her lips from his, she mumbled, "So long. Love me, Padraig."

"It will be my pleasure, my lady." He laughed, stepped back, and bowed to her. "May I assist you with your shoes, my queen?"

Laughing together, the two tugged off her slippers and woolen hose, and when they all fell to the floor, she fell onto the bed in her chemise. This was why she adored him so. He could always make her laugh, make her forget all the difficult parts of her life.

He'd already dropped his plaid, so she knelt up on the bed and reached for his tunic, shoving it up to his shoulders, as high as she could reach. He finished for her, yanking it over his head just before her lips found his nipples, teasing him the way he did her, raking her teeth across each one until he said, "Enough torture, my lady."

He picked her up so fast that she shrieked, but he settled her into the bed carefully, helping her remove her chemise before climbing in next to her. He cupped her cheek, and his expression sobered.

"No more laughing. I've waited for this to happen for too long, Gisela. The thought of you gets me up in the morn, gives me a reason to breathe. I love you, and I'm so sorry I didn't see a future for us so clearly before."

"Just kiss me, Padraig. We can talk later."

His lips descended to hers, ravaging her, and he angled his mouth to deepen the kiss, working her into a froth of need, her panting coming so quickly it astonished her. His mouth trailed a path of kisses to her ear then down her neck, before it fell lower, kisses landing in the valley of her breasts before settling on one, suckling until her nipple peaked. She moaned with pleasure, the heat of his body against hers the most natural and wonderful feeling of all.

He settled himself between her legs, teasing her junction with the tip of his arousal, her need for him to be inside her nearly unbearable.

"Padraig, please." But he didn't let up, continuing to tease, advancing and retreating while he tasted her other breast. Her hands moved to his back, fingers digging into his corded muscles then descending to the curve of his buttocks. At long last he finally entered her, stopping short filling her. Her lusty sigh was so loud she might be embarrassed, but she wasn't.

He stopped his movement and whispered, "You

wish to tease me with your sweet sounds? You do, like no other, with every sigh and moan, my lady," Padraig muttered, his mouth still occupied with her breast. "I need you like no other. We belong together. Do you agree with me, Gisela? I think we should marry on the morrow."

"Aye, please, Padraig. I will marry you whenever you like, just finish this. I need you all the way inside me. Stop your teasing, I beg you! I cannot stand it any longer." With each beat of her pulse, he moved inside her farther, her slickness welcoming him, encouraging him.

But then he stopped, forcing her to beg again. "Please, Padraig, harder."

"Gisela, you are the one for me. I know it. Together we will do wonderful things."

"Padraig!" she pinched his arm. "Now!"

With a grin, he pulled all the way back out before he plunged fully inside her, their rhythm building but not enough to satisfy her. She pushed back, moving against him until he hit her hard where she needed it most, helping him establish their rhythm. It apparently satisfied him as much as it did her, from his low growl of pleasure. He let her set the pace, and she was amazed with how well they fit together. Her need built to a pinnacle that she couldn't go over, and as if he knew just what she needed, he reached between them and caressed the perfect spot. She tumbled over the edge with a scream of his name, her hands gripping his shoulders as she climaxed.

Her climax pushed him until he roared out his own climax. When her pants slowed, she sighed happily.

She didn't know lovemaking could be this good.

———————◆———————

They lay quietly in each other's arms, Gisela tucked against him and Padraig running a finger down the curve of her arm.

"I don't ever wish to see that man again."

"You won't have to. He's dead."

"He is? In battle? Who killed him?" Her questions came at him in a rush, but he decided some things were better left unsaid, this treasured time together too sacred to be poisoned by such a discussion.

He put his finger up against her lips. "Hush, lass. He's dead. Whatever was happening inside his head may have killed him as quickly as any man's sword. Shall we never mention him again?"

She relaxed against him, pausing for a moment. "Yes, please. I never want to hear his name again."

"But there is still one piece missing. I must ask how you escaped him. You don't know how happy I was to see you running freely instead of tied up somewhere. Where were you?"

She sighed, playing with the dark hairs on his arm. "First he had me tied in a cottage in the forest somewhere. I was there for days. But my guess is that news that the Grant warriors were coming scared him. That was when he took me to his castle. His father wanted to hold me in the keep, and they fought. He tied me up, gagged me, and left me inside the granary." She shivered. "It was creepy. That's where the adder was. It crawled out from beneath the grain sacks."

"Och, lassie, but you are a strong one. Some lasses would faint. How did you get free of the bindings?"

"As the adder moved closer, I managed to wriggle my way around the building, as far away from the slithering beast as I could." She closed her eyes and shivered again.

"No snakes here," he assured her, kissing her forehead. "And if one shows up, I'll kill it before ever you see it."

"I know." She smiled up at him, then held one wrist up to the dim moonlight, showing him where she'd cut them. "My good fortune prevailed, and I found a small dagger near one of the sacks, probably used to cut them open. I managed to cut the bindings—and nicked my skin just a bit, too, I was trembling so." She shook her head and stared at the doorway. "I'm amazed at the strength I found at the sight of that adder. Once I was free, I crept out of the building and nearly into the battle. I slipped out the back door in the curtain wall—it was wide open, for some reason. Then I just ran, finding my way around the castle and toward home. And there you found me."

He kissed the wound on her wrist softly. "Well done. Now for the important question. Will your brothers allow you to marry me? We are handfasted, so we will marry, but I wish to have your brothers' support."

"I think so. This has been difficult for all of us,

and I don't wish to wait. Padraig, I've thought hard on what I want for my life, and while I love my niece and nephew, they have a new mama they adore. Marcas is working hard to grow the clan, and with the help of the Grants and Ramsays, I think we'll be successful. And now that man is no longer a threat…"

"What are you trying to say, lass?"

"I'm saying that I could happily live wherever you wish to, Padraig. I'll follow you wherever you go. And if you wish for us to live on Grant land, I would be willing as long as we promise to travel to Black Isle for regular visits."

He caressed the soft skin on the back of her hand. "I had an idea for what I'd like us to do. While I was imprisoned in the cell…"

"Imprisoned?" She nearly sat up but he set his hand on her chest, encouraging her back to where she was.

"Aye. I'll tell you my story later. All that matters for now is that I got out and am here with you. In the cell with me was a surgeon from England. He told me about a physician in London who only works with children. Have you ever heard of such a thing?"

"Nay, but you would be wonderful at it. You should do it." She stared up at him, and he could see the love and excitement dancing across her beautiful face.

"You think so?"

"Haven't you told me you worked with your mother?"

"Aye, on many occasions. Gracie always helped,

too, but she wasn't always available. Why do you think I would be good at it? My mother believes so, too, but I want your opinion." Sometimes he thought this would work, but he needed her support in this endeavor.

"Because you are so wonderful with bairns. And I love the idea." Her excitement was bubbling over as she told him about her adventure with Tara and the ill bairns, and he couldn't help but wonder if his finding her on Black Isle had been destiny all along.

"What are you thinking? I can see the glitter in your eyes." Padraig said with a smile.

"We can do it together. You could become a physician, and I'll help you. But we only work with bairns. What do you think?"

Padraig paused, considering her words. Then he leaned down to kiss her. "'Tis a brilliant idea. I can think of none other I'd rather partner with. We'll figure it out as we go. We have many healers close to my clan to learn from, even Brigid, Jennet, and Tara."

Padraig had never been happier. His life had direction, something that truly excited him. A wonderful wife and a chosen path working with bairns.

It was perfect.

CHAPTER TWENTY-THREE

———— ◆ ————

GISELA HAD NEVER been happier. She had thought lying in Padraig's arms after making love had been her happiest moment, but now that she was about to marry the man she adored, she realized she'd been wrong. She thought her insides would burst with happiness. She'd given her family only one day to prepare for the wedding, because she was not going to wait any longer to marry this amazing man.

And that day was finally here.

Kara came up to her and said, "Do I look pwetty, Auntie 'Ela?" Gisela smiled at the wee lass dressed in a pale blue gown with dark blue ribbons on the bodice, silver threading shining in the light. "It sparkles. See?" She wiggled her chest back and forth with a giggle.

"Aye, my sweet. You look beautiful in your gown. Brigid chose the perfect blue for you, did she not?"

"You're pwetty, too. I like gween."

Gisela kissed her niece, lifting her for a little twirl as Marcas stepped into her chamber.

"Lass, you are beautiful. I wish Mama and Papa

were here to see and celebrate with us."

Kara ran over to her father, and he picked her up, settling her in his arms.

"They are here with us, Marcas," Gisela said, unable to stop the misting in her gaze. "I know it to be true. Thank you for agreeing to the wedding so quickly. I know this is the right thing. I love Padraig with all my heart. He's such a good man."

"I agree," he said, leaning down to kiss her cheek. "You've chosen well, and you've chosen a good purpose for your life together. I look forward to hearing tales of your work and travels."

"I hope you aren't upset that we plan to leave for a wee bit."

"Not at all. You deserve all the happiness in the world after what you've been through." He set Kara down and straightened the skirt on her pale blue gown. "Are you ready? 'Tis time to start."

Gisela nodded, ecstatic that her wedding day had arrived. She smoothed her light green skirt, straightened the gold ribbons on the dark green bodice, then sighed happily and reached for her brother's arm.

He led the two of them down the stairs and onto the front steps of the keep. As they watched, a formation of horses and riders came their way, all but one stopping midway. Padraig, grinning wider than she'd ever seen, urged his black horse straight to her.

Her lovely white horse came behind him, her mane braided with pink ribbons. Behind her came Marcas's horse. He would ride ahead of the couple as chieftain of the clan, and Kara had wheedled him into letting her ride with him.

When Padraig reached the steps, he turned his horse sideways and bent toward her, a bow from horseback. "My lady," he whispered with a wink.

Marcas said, "Why are you here, Grant? You should be awaiting us at the firth. Trying to rush things, are you?" He mounted his horse and waited for Alvery to hand his daughter up to him. She clapped her hands with excitement, giggling once she settled on her father's lap.

"My lord," Padraig said, losing his smirk, "if you don't mind, I proposed to her on horseback so I wish to ride with her to the firth on horseback."

Gisela couldn't stop her giggle, so Marcas relented and said, "Fine. We'll see you at the firth."

Padraig hopped down, then scooped her up and settled her on her mare sideways, giving her time to arrange her skirts. Once she was secure, he mounted his own horse and turned, waiting for her mount to come abreast of his, and they rode across the courtyard between rows of clan members, both Grant and Matheson, cheering them on. He cued Midnight Blue to bow as he passed Jake, his laird, and do a quick pirouette in front of his mother and father, his brother next to them. The clan roared their approval.

"Are you happy, lass?" Padraig asked as they reached the gate, flung wide in celebration.

"So happy, Padraig."

They made their way to the spot they'd chosen on the firth for their wedding. Gisela was surprised to see the area so beautifully decorated, and she was quite sure she had Padraig's cousins to thank for all the hard work. The sky was unusually blue, and the sunshine brightened every one of the dozens—hundreds—of flowers around them. She dismounted slowly, taking the time to appreciate all the details. A log sat across the front near the firth, covered with a beautiful arrangement of intertwining vines and wildflowers. A glorious display of color had been arranged in pots around the small clearing, the whites, yellows, and pinks a testament to the beauty of summer. Brigid handed bouquets of bluebells to both Kara and Gisela, and Gisela embraced her sister-in-law—sister, truly—to show her gratitude for all they'd done to make her wedding perfect. Tears misted in her gaze, and she feared she was about to cry through her own wedding.

"Stop it, my dear sister," Brigid said with a kiss to Gisela's cheek. "Go on, now. 'Tis time."

But she should have known Padraig wouldn't allow her to weep for long.

Padraig's laird Jamie set the stage for the event.

Once they were all in place, Jamie strode over and handed Padraig a big bouquet of thistles, the purple tops beautiful. Everyone knew what lay beneath the stunning color. Gisela stared at Padraig to see how he would react. He didn't take it right away, aware the prickly plant would leave its mark, but Jamie said, "Take it. One of Clan Grant's many traditions I'm passing down to you." His cousin couldn't hide his smirk over the deed either.

The Grants, the ones who had managed to arrive in time to celebrate with them all, broke into applause, so Padraig did what he did best. He took the bouquet in hand and made a big production of the thistles hurting him.

Starting with a roar of pain, he tossed the bouquet back and forth from one hand to the other, howling, jumping, and acting out for all the bairns in the group, even tripping once and falling, the bouquet landing in his lap. Kara and Tiernay roared with delight while Alasdair, Els, and Alick laughed as they ran in circles watching Padraig. Dyna shook her head watching all the theatrics.

But Gisela's tears were now replaced with laughter as he tipped her a wink. He wrapped a borrowed shawl around the stems to protect his hand and stood next to her. "Are you ready, love?"

She nodded, wiping a tear of joy from her eye.

He whispered loud enough for all to hear, "Why don't you hold this bouquet, Gisela? 'Tis quite lovely."

Kara barked out a quick, "Nay. Auntie!"

She shook her head, breaking into laughter again while the bairns all filled the air with their giggles and shouts, holding up her bouquet of bluebells to show him.

"Trade?" he asked, a wide grin on his face.

She shook her head more slowly this time, so he turned to face the priest.

Father MacKintyre moved in closer to begin the ceremony, but Gisela heard very little.

She set her head on Padraig's shoulder and giggled all the way through their wedding, various members of the congregation laughing along with her joy.

Their wedding was perfect.

EPILOGUE

———◆———

Two months later…

PADRAIG PUSHED HIS chair back from the trestle table, his belly full from the evening meal. He glanced around the Cameron great hall, one of his favorite places because he'd spent much time training here with Uncle Aedan's brother, Ruari. He and Gisela had arrived the day before, having already spent time with his mother at Grant Castle and Aunt Brenna at Ramsay Castle, reviewing things he'd already known and learning new skills they'd need as healers. He noticed Gisela doing the same thing, the view of the hall in the evening with all the torches drawing her attention as much as it had his.

He said, "Aunt Jennie, your extra touches are lovely. The tapestries of all the castles are so well done. I'd never taken the time to study them before."

Uncle Aedan drawled, "You were too busy with your antics back then, trying to impress all the lasses."

Gisela arched a brow at him but said nothing.

He shrugged his shoulders sheepishly. "I guess I was a wee bit randy back then, but only because you were not here, wife."

She laughed at his back-handed compliment.

"Thank you, Padraig," Aunt Jennie said. "We worked hard on them over many months, and they are quite popular."

Padraig stared at the grouping on the largest wall, unable to tear his gaze from it. His aunt and cousins had done a fine job capturing the essence of each castle. Grant Castle sat high on its hill, while Ramsay Castle's beauty was reflected in the nearby loch. They'd placed a small design of the Lochluin Abbey in the background of Cameron Castle, probably because it was such a large part of their lives.

Gisela said, "I recognize Cameron, Grant, and Ramsay, but I don't know the fourth castle." She looked to her husband and asked, "Have we been there yet?"

"Nay, no healers there. 'Tis Castle Curanta, my cousin Loki's castle."

"I guess you'll not see it until your return from London," Aunt Jennie said. "I do hope you'll share everything you learn. I would love to know what the physicians in England say about treating bairns. I don't know if anyone has thought to treat them differently, other than giving them smaller doses of our potions. The two of you will work wonders together."

Riley, Tara's sister, burst into the hall and joined them on the dais, her eyes wide. "I hope you're ready for a wonderful show. I'm quite impressed by the detail in their plan."

"Whose plan?" Gisela whispered to her husband. "What show?"

Padraig had been leaning back quite lazily in his chair, but he straightened at Riley's words. The sparkle in his aunt's eyes made him wary.

Someone had something up their sleeve.

Aunt Jennie couldn't contain her smirk. "Gisela, I'm not sure if Padraig has told you, but he fostered here as a youth, spending most of his time with Ruari, Aedan's brother, and the two were inseparable for a long time."

"And Padraig was quite the trickster," Riley added, standing behind her mother. "His favorite thing to do was to mimic others, especially lasses."

Gisela looked at her husband and burst into laughter. "Padraig, you are about to be embarrassed, or so I'm guessing. What say you? Do they have good reason to tease you?"

Hellfire, but they surely did, and he couldn't begin to deny it.

Ruari's wife, Juliana, came in first. She walked in a circle around the hall, her voice raised so all could hear. "For those of you who don't remember, Padraig's favorite thing to do was to pretend he was a lass. He used to mimic me and my walk to Ruari, claiming it was the main thing Ruari was entranced by."

She stepped up to the dais and said, "And now, we have a few who will mimic Padraig."

The small crowd erupted in giggles, clapping a bit but falling to silent attention when they heard the door open.

Ruari was first, in a purple gown with pink slippers, and he pranced around the hall using Padraig's words. "Sometimes I think all you think on is lasses, Ruari. Can you not stop staring at Juliana?"

Brin, Aedan's son, came in next, wearing a blue Ramsay plaid slung over his shoulder. "Arghh, what in hellfire do you think you're doing? Are you a walking fool?"

"Who is he imitating?" Gisela whispered to Padraig.

Padraig rolled his eyes and said, "Logan Ramsay." Then he yelled out, "He was so easy to mimic!"

Others came through, one at a time, and Gisela wiped tears of laughter from her eyes. "Padraig, you were a true rogue. How many others did you tease?"

The entire hall shouted back at her. "Everyone! He teased everyone."

After the applause for the performers, Ruari came forward and handed Gisela a huge bouquet of flowers. "I present these to you as a sympathy bouquet, lass. We feel sorry for all you'll have to endure living with Padraig. It will be a trial at times, so you'll need something to help brighten up your spirits."

The group applauded again and cheered as Padraig finally stood and tugged his wife up next to him. He wrapped his arm around her and said, "Thank you, everyone. I take these jests as the blessing they are. Just remember, Ruari Cameron, I never forget these things. And I'll be back just for you."

The group roared its approval.

Gisela giggled and laughed and leaned over to say, "I do love you so, even as a prankster, Padraig."

"I'm grateful," he said. "I was afraid you'd run away after that performance."

"Never," she said, grasping his hand. "I'll always be by your side."

"And I look forward to every moment with you."

———————◆———————

Outside the curtain wall of Cameron Castle, two people on horseback listened to the cheering going on inside the walls.

"What do you wish to do now? They're married and happy. I don't think you'll separate them."

"Mayhap not. I don't like the way these clans all became involved in our business on Black Isle. These two will be traveling so they'll be no threat, but the others, I'm not so sure. I don't want to ever see a Grant or Ramsay on Black Isle again."

"What are you talking about?"

One gave the other an evil grin. "We still have a relative of the Grants on Black isle, Tara Cameron. Marcas will never take his eye from his bride, and Ethan's woman is someone I don't trust. But the third lass is free."

"What do you have in mind?"

"You'll see. Back to Black Isle we go. We have one last chance to destroy the Mathesons for good. Their fate is in my hands. I'm not sure exactly what I'll do, but I can assure you, I'll not fail this time."

D EAR READER,
Thank you for reading Gisela and Padraig's story! If you wish to learn more about Ruari and Juliana's story, you'll find it in The Banished Highlander. Since Ruari wasn't a Grant or Ramsay, I released it as a stand-alone novel. If you missed it, get your copy here at Amazon.

There is one more story left in this series about Tara and Shaw, but I'm sure you guessed that already.

I researched the first official physician in Scotland and came upon the name of the Beatons. In early history, many members of Clann Meic-bethad (in Gaelic, a good illustration as to why I don't use the official Gaelic names) or Clan MacBeth. They began practicing medicine in the early fourteenth century, so I didn't think it was a stretch that a relative of their clan named de Bethune would have been wandering around the Highlands in the late thirteenth century.

Once again, everything I write is fiction, so the name John de Bethune is fiction as is my referral to pediatric doctors and brain tumors.

Happy reading!

Keira Montclair

keiramontclair@gmail.com
www.keiramontclair.com
http://facebook.com/KeiraMontclair/
http://www.pinterest.com/KeiraMontclair/

NOVELS BY KEIRA MONTCLAIR

JAMIE AND GRACIE-Book Seven
SORCHA-Book Eight
KYLA-Book Nine
BETHIA-Book Ten
LOKI'S CHRISTMAS STORY-Book Eleven
ELIZABETH-Book Twelve

THE BAND OF COUSINS
HIGHLAND VENGEANCE
HIGHLAND ABDUCTION
HIGHLAND RETRIBUTION
HIGHLAND LIES
HIGHLAND FORTITUDE
HIGHLAND RESILIENCE
HIGHLAND DEVOTION
HIGHLAND BRAWN
HIGHLAND YULETIDE MAGIC

HIGHLAND SWORDS
THE SCOT'S BETRAYAL
THE SCOT'S SPY
THE SCOT'S PURSUIT
THE SCOT'S QUEST
THE SCOT'S DECEPTION
THE SCOT'S ANGEL

HIGHLAND HEALERS
THE CURSE OF BLACK ISLE
THE WITCH OF BLACK ISLE
THE SCOURGE OF BLACK ISLE

THE SOULMATE CHRONICLES
#1 TRUSTING A HIGHLANDER

#2 TRUSTING A SCOT

STAND-ALONE BOOKS
THE BANISHED HIGHLANDER
REFORMING THE DUKE-REGENCY
WOLF AND THE WILD SCOTS
FALLING FOR THE CHIEFTAIN-3RD in a
collaborative trilogy

THE SUMMERHILL SERIES-
CONTEMPORARY ROMANCE
#1-ONE SUMMERHILL DAY
#2-A FRESH START FOR TWO
#3-THREE REASONS TO LOVE

ABOUT THE AUTHOR

Keira Montclair is the pen name of an author who lives in South Carolina with her husband. She loves to write fast-paced, emotional romance, especially with children as secondary characters.

When she's not writing, she loves to spend time with her grandchildren. She's worked as a high school math teacher, a registered nurse, and an office manager. She loves ballet, mathematics, puzzles, learning anything new, and creating new characters for her readers to fall in love with.

She writes historical romantic suspense. Her bestselling series is a family saga that follows two medieval Scottish clans through four generations and now numbers over thirty books.

Contact her through her website:
www.keiramontclair.com